PENGUIN ANANDA
THE PATH OF LIGHT

Renuka Narayanan is an author and columnist with the *Hindustan Times*.

ALSO BY THE AUTHOR

The Book of Prayer
The Little Book of Indian Wisdom

The Path *of* Light

Tales from the Upanishads, Jatakas and Indic Folklore

RENUKA NARAYANAN

PENGUIN
ANANDA
An imprint of Penguin Random House

PENGUIN ANANDA

USA | Canada | UK | Ireland | Australia
New Zealand | India | South Africa | China | Singapore

Penguin Ananda is part of the Penguin Random House group of companies
whose addresses can be found at global.penguinrandomhouse.com

Published by Penguin Random House India Pvt. Ltd
4th Floor, Capital Tower 1, MG Road,
Gurugram 122 002, Haryana, India

First published in Penguin Ananda by Penguin Random House India 2017

10 9 8 7 6 5 4 3 2

The views and opinions expressed in this book are the author's own and
the facts are as reported by her which have been verified to the extent
possible, and the publishers are not in any way liable for the same.

ISBN 9780143428558

Typeset in Bell MT by Manipal Digital Systems, Manipal

Printed at Repro India Limited

www.penguin.co.in

MIX
Paper from
responsible sources
FSC® C047271

This is a legitimate digitally printed version of the book and therefore might not
have certain extra finishing on the cover.

For Ponni,
my first storyteller

Contents

Contents

Introduction

Dear Reader,

Welcome to this collection of old Indian stories, with a few from South East Asia. I have retold them because I found them moving, amusing or extraordinary. They happened to come my way, touched a chord and allowed me elbow room as a modern storyteller.

I lack the words to properly express my wonder at the vast heritage of Indian storytelling—its depth and range, its inventiveness and subtle in-house cues. For instance, while retelling the story of Pingala, the Pretty Woman, by Vyasa, it suddenly struck me that the tale could have been set in any city in any one of the mahajanapadas or major nation states of ancient India. But by being set in Videha, the city of 'Vaidehi Sita', Pingala's story is textured with ironic depth. Realizing the world of unstated significance in that location made me feel close to the subversive mind of that master storyteller who delighted in chiaroscuro, in playing with shades and contrasts. It was a personal Vyasa moment, as hundreds of thousands of people have had before me, and always will.

The supernatural may flit in and out of the events described here but after all, these stories are from the 'mysterious East'. Gods, yakshas, nagas and kinnaras stroll about as though they own the place, which in fact, they do. This is their conceptual home and they're not going anywhere that we can tell. Why, we would be bereft without them and the exciting interface that they vivify between the known and the unknown. You could call it 'magic realism', and be spot on.

If the stories in this book have a common thread it is their all too human component. They take me through some of the dilemmas and debates that beset our adventures as frail beings on the rocky road of life. Sometimes it's a misstep we take and sometimes the sky falls on our heads. These old stories are very much about the kind of responses possible to us in various tricky situations and to each other, which is why I find them so interesting, as I hope you will.

1

Silliness is, well, silly

They say that the Sakyamuni Gautama Buddha was not just tall, strong and handsome, but that he spoke very well in a low, clear voice. There were points, after all, to being raised royal and having had the very best teachers that his father, King Suddhodana, could entice to the locked pleasure park of Gautama's youth at Kapilavastu.

The things the Sakyamuni said were so simple yet so interesting that the cleverest people were not the least bit bored, and the simplest people did not feel his words fly right over their heads, while the largest and the most difficult group to please, the middlebrow, felt his words were just right;

they were neither condescended to nor fatigued by having to keep up with one metaphysical hair being split into seventy-six. Pitching it just so was the secret of many a great guru's success and the Goddess Sarasvati, the deity of arts and learning had evidently marked the Sakyamuni as one of her own.

The concept of reincarnation is the thread for the Jatakas, or tales of the Buddha's previous lives before he was born as Siddhartha, prince of the Sakyas, and attained Buddhahood in that birth. He is called the Bodhisattva or pre-Buddha in his previous lives.

In one such birth, when the Bodhisattva was a trader and not a prince, he had to pass by a village on the outskirts of the city of Varanasi, to which he was headed on work. He happened to notice in the village a carpenter with a bald head, hammering away at a door frame of stout teak. Just then, a bloodthirsty mosquito lighted on the carpenter's gleaming pate and stung him on his bare scalp.

'Rid me of this!' he roared at his son, who was splitting wood for kindling nearby and was not very bright. The son promptly swung his axe at the insect, splitting his father's skull into two. 'Better a clever enemy than a foolish well-wisher,' thought the Bodhisattva as he walked away, which amounts to saying that sometimes we invite disaster where we seek relief from the foolish.

In another Jataka, a tortoise refused to leave its pond one extra severe Indian summer, although it was clear that the environment was drying up. The fish and crabs and frogs had migrated to safety through a small water channel that still remained, but the tortoise dug itself in because it was too fond of its comfort zone and absolutely refused to read the signs. Soon, there was no way left to escape from the dwindled pond but the tortoise merely wriggled deeper into the last bit of damp earth. The Bodhisattva, who was a potter in this story, went to the remains of the pond one day to get a fresh load of raw material. His spade cracked the tortoise's shell for it looked just like a lump of clay and the tortoise cried aloud in pain. 'Serves me right for not quitting when I had the chance,' it said (or the equivalent in Prakrit) and died repenting. The Bodhisattva used this unfortunate incident to show the danger of not letting go when you have to, of too much attachment to things like family, home, money, position and power, of clinging to something that is familiar even though it is clearly bad for you.

To reinforce this point in a different way, there's another Jataka that tells of four silly princes of Varanasi and the tesu tree (*Butea monosperma*, in case of surpassing interest), also famous as the dhak and the palash; or as the flame of the forest, whose brilliant orange flowers are used even today to make coloured dye to smear everyone with on Holi, the Festival of Colours. King Brahmadatta, the father of these four silly princes, was fed up with his sons, each one of whom seemed more doltish than the other. They were getting on for fourteen, almost men by ancient Indian reckoning, but they still fought like babies and paid no attention to their teachers, nor did they seem aware of their impending duties as princes—although they were fully acquainted with each and every one of their many rights.

Their father wanted to teach them some common sense and conspired with the Bodhisattva, born this time as the king's trusty charioteer. First told all kinds of fanciful tales about the tesu tree, the princes were then nudged by the king to ask the charioteer to show them one. The Bodhisattva took the oldest to see the tesu when it had just put forth new leaves of the most tender, delicate green. He took the second prince to see the tesu when its leaves were dark green and spread protectively over the buds in budding season. He took the third prince to see the tesu in its full glory of triumphant flowers, while the fourth prince got to see it only when the flowering was all done and nothing remained on the tesu but hard brown pods. The princes were given over so wholly to the pursuit of pleasure and had so little curiosity and interest in anything beyond their daily gratification that they never thought to discuss these little field trips or to compare notes.

The king had counted on this, and when all four were done with tesu sighting, he set the princes up for fine and thorough public disgrace.

5

He commanded their presence in court at a levee, on the pretext that they were getting to be big boys and needed to take an interest in their public duties. Having dressed up and marched in proudly, the princes were arranged on small golden seats around the king, where all the assembled praja could see them. There was a good representation of subjects: all the nobility was there, of course, and the nagar seths or big merchants of immense wealth, and by special invitation, so were the heads of every trading, craftsmen's and professional guild along with five guild members each, and hoi polloi of every kind. Even the most famous and beautiful of the nagar vadhus or public women had taken their place, determined not to miss whatever was going to happen, for word had spread in Varanasi that the four silly princes, a blot on their fair and blessed city, were going to be made a spectacle of by their desperate father.

Looking at the foolish, trusting faces of his stupid sons, King Brahmadatta suffered a tiny fatherly pang for what he was about to do, but knew very well that his duty as king came first.

After the customary opening formalities of a royal court (the oboes blew slightly off-key in excitement but only the nagar vadhus noticed), the king introduced the princes to the praja and got down to the unpleasant task at hand.

'To assure the public of your worthiness, demonstrate your powers of observation. Tell them, for instance, what a tesu tree looks like,' he said invitingly. Of course, they were unable to agree and after they had been soundly booed by the scandalized public of Varanasi for their entirely unbecoming and utterly dangerous silliness, they were told sternly to always get the whole picture and see a situation from all angles.

2

The gold beneath the grime

Eons ago, says a Jataka, there was a very rich merchant family in a proud and noble city somewhere in the Upper Gangetic Plain. The family lived in great splendour in their magnificent townhouse with its big, inner courtyard and its own temple. The house was surrounded by acres of garden with fragrant thickets of jasmine and golden champaka flowers and one end of the property rejoiced in several big cowsheds with at least 200 cows in them. The family gave generously to orphans and to homeless people, to the king's hospice and to the charitable projects of temples. They supported poor students and indigent widows and contributed handsomely to the upkeep and running of rest houses for travellers and pilgrims. They often went to their pleasant country estate upriver, where they had swings and hammocks put up in the mango orchards. They picnicked on the riverbank and bathed in the river and had races and played ball, took out their boats, gossiped, napped, played long games of pachisi, had moonlit suppers, sang songs and told stories—all three generations together of grandparents, uncles, aunts, cousins and faithful retainers.

However, the fortunes of this family became greatly reduced and not just that, all the men of the family died one by one. The servants went away to find other work and only an old grandmother and a little granddaughter were left. They escaped starvation by hiring themselves out as domestic workers and since they were too old and too young respectively to cook whole meals for others, the only things they could do, for which they were paid accordingly, were a bit of cleaning and light kitchen work, like peeling and cutting vegetables, washing and drying the whole spices, picking rice and lentils clean and helping to make pickles and papads. It was a big comedown for those who had been waited on all their lives and had never lacked for anything—but they were glad not to have to beg.

At this time, the Bodhisattva was a trader who sometimes worked in the city with another trader. This business partner was secretly less scrupulous than the Bodhisattva and naturally, the Bodhisattva did not know that. Their agreement was to divide the town into territories and enter each other's areas only after the other one had left it. One day, the greedy trader came down the former fine family's street, crying aloud his wares that included rare and costly trinkets like necklaces of foreign coins, coral strings from the Coromandel and chains of fine glass beads in colours as varied as the sea from across the Eastern Ocean.

Now nearly eight years old, the little granddaughter had been taught her manners since she was barely two. She missed her mother

11

and father very much, having lost them both to a boat wreck on the river. But she managed not to complain about having to work so hard and at such dull, tiring tasks one after the other; nor did she complain about not having enough to eat or about wearing ugly hand-me-downs or about being spoken to crossly by the spoilt sons and daughters of the houses she worked in. Doing so would have embarrassed her grandmother and so she said nothing at all and never asked for anything, letting her small face crumple in tears only when there was nobody around to see.

But an instinct for fine things was in her blood and when she saw the trader's lovely necklaces, she suddenly longed for an ornament, for something pretty all her own, and begged her grandmother to trade whatever she could. Touched to be asked to do something by the child, the grandmother went off to rummage in the storeroom at the back of their crumbling family home. She noticed a grimy old bowl lying in a corner with other old household bric-a-brac and offered that to the trader for a modest bead necklace.

One discreet scratch with a needle and the greedy trader knew that he held a bowl made of solid gold. Plotting instantly to get it for almost nothing, he threw it back saying that it was too worthless to trade and waited expectantly for the old lady to beg him to take it. But the old lady did no such thing, for such a move simply did not occur to her. Instead, she nodded quietly and withdrew abashed, little realizing that it was the old payasa, or milk pudding, bowl of the head of their family that had been put away after his death and had become unrecognizably dirty. She touched her granddaughter's hair gently in apology and the little girl blinked hard and stoically spoke of something else.

When the Bodhisattva, the good trader, came by a couple of hours later after his wily business partner had left, the little girl did not dare accost him for fear of another snub. But since he swung a whole handful of necklaces at her in the jolliest way and smiled kindly, she asked him to wait and went in to ask her grandmother to try her luck again at trade. The old lady came out with the same old bowl, handed it to the trader and sent the little girl to shut the storeroom door so as to leave them alone for a minute. When the little girl ran in, the grandmother whispered to the trader that she knew her goods were worthless but pleaded with him to do the best he could, to give a very simple necklace or at least a bead bangle in exchange.

'But who told you this bowl was worthless?' asked the astonished trader, giving it a good rub and showing her the shine. Not only did he give them a fair deal for the golden bowl, but he also obligingly paid cash for other things of value discovered in the storeroom. He went away with a clear conscience, receiving many blessings from the grandmother and a beaming namaste from the granddaughter for the warm blanket suddenly obtained against cold fate.

The greedy trader collapsed and died of rage when he found out.

While the good trader was, of course, the Bodhisattva, the greedy trader who was not above trying to cheat widows and orphans was the Buddha's wicked cousin Devdatt, and this was the beginning of Devdatt's grudge against the Buddha through many rebirths thereafter, carrying mountains of baggage and never being at peace for a moment in all those lifetimes.

3

The royal horse

There's a little-known Jataka that seems at first to be a 'So what?' sort of story until the point bites home. It also tells us that in the old days, people could be made to feel ashamed through a simple story because it mattered to them to be respectable and well-thought-of for the right reasons. This story tells of an ancient kingdom in India, even before the Buddha's time in the sixth century BCE. It was a well-ruled and tightly administered kingdom in which the king's favourite horse was taken every day to bathe in a special pool. Even by ancient standards, this was a lovely, clean pool where pink lotuses and mauve water lilies grew in attractive clusters and swans sailed about in intense, loving pairs. Every monsoon, the lovelorn chakora bird called despairingly and untiringly to its impossibly distant amour, the moon, and fat, golden carp darted about in fearless play.

The lake was in the royal preserve and poachers and picnickers had been given fair warning— du-du-dum-dum, dum-dum-dum-dum—by the town crier and his drummer to stay away. Even the drummer's donkey, if caught trespassing, would be fed with the other culprits to the crocodiles in the lake, while the ever-ready public jeered heartlessly at them for having sought such stupid deaths, all for the sake of unlicensed fish. All told, the king's favourite horse enjoyed his daily dip very much.

But one day, the horse absolutely refused to enter the lake. It dug its heels in and rolled its eyes wildly, shook its proud head and tossed its silky mane, much to the surprise of the royal grooms. When clucks, pleas and protestations failed and they tried to drag the horse into the lake, it threw a dangerous equine tantrum and had to be led back to its stable, where it sulked and refused to take its feed. What the grooms did not realize, but the horse did, was that a filthy, newly caught horse had just been washed in the lake and its odour still lingered in the waters. The fastidious royal horse refused to enter the polluted water despite the coaxing of the perplexed grooms and had finally lost its temper, and they totally failed to understand why.

When the news was carried to the palace, the king sent an astute minister to investigate. Wise in the ways of animals and not lacking in plain common sense either, the minister looked at the water, smelled the air and straightaway deduced why the royal horse had resisted getting into the water. Inquiry confirmed his observation. The minister advised the grooms to take the royal horse elsewhere for a day or two until the smell faded and all was well. The lesson the Jataka patently wished to teach was, 'When animals value cleanliness, should human beings lag behind?'

4

The sixth weapon and the
sticky ghoul

A curious little Jataka tells of the importance of
mental agility or rather, self-control and focus.
These sharpen the wits whereby many an opponent
or obstacle can be overcome. This Jataka, with
its elaborate build-up, may take its time getting
to the point but those were the days of oil lamps
and scary shadows, just right for a long, ghoulish
yet moral tale. In this story, the Bodhisattva was
born as a prince of Varanasi and 800 fortune
tellers predicted over his hapless baby head that
he would be a great warrior 'with mastery over
the five weapons'—which we, like those before us,

do not require diagrams to decode as the good old Panchendri or the Five Senses, those built-in snares by which each one of us is led astray. So they named the prince 'Panchaastra', meaning 'Five Weapons' in Sanskrit, in affirmation that he would perfectly control these five weapons used by Nature against Spirit, and would even turn the Panchendri into weapons of his own.

In due course, the prince was sent for even higher learning than could be obtained in his already great home town to an accomplished guru of the age. The guru lived north by northwest of Varanasi at Takshashila, which was famous then for enlightened teachers. After a pleasant and useful stay at Takshashila, the prince set off homewards to Varanasi carrying five wonderful weapons gifted by his guru, becoming literally a 'Panchaastra' now in addition to his mastery of the Five Senses.

Entering a dark jungle, the prince, in the best classical tradition, was at once treated to a perfect concert of blood-curdling howls. When these horrific sounds that made even his princely hair stand on end died away to a moment of menacing silence, he was straightaway, and with vigour, set upon by a man-eating ghoul, whom the Jataka reliably informs us had a particularly nasty nature and also had sticky hair, staring eyes and an unpleasantly mottled belly. Perfectly cool and calm—a credit to both his horoscope and his high-level training—the prince unleashed one weapon after the other, but everything that he sent flying at his foe merely stuck to the ghoul's hair and body. Finally, he attacked him with his fists and found that he, too, was firmly stuck. While the ghoul, though determined not to forgo lunch, privately wondered at the prince's courage, the prince remembered the guru he had left behind and sure enough, was rewarded with a thought.

'My greatest weapon is still unused,' he calmly proceeded to inform the ghoul. 'It is a diamond-edged weapon, lodged inside me by my guru's extraordinary powers. If you eat me, it will tear your guts apart from within. So there.'

Greatly impressed, if not by fear of a fancy astra then certainly by the prince's bravado, the ghoul freed the prince and sent him on his way with false bright promises to desist thereafter from being a threat to the populace. The prince mentally saluted his guru for teaching him how to think his way out of a fix when all else had failed—the greatest weapon of all.

5

The lake of lotuses

There's a Jataka that tells whomsoever it may concern that the rules go back a long way about not only doing the right thing but also being seen doing the right thing. It's the strangely familiar story of Prince Subhash, meaning 'well spoken', and Prince Sashi, meaning 'moon', who had a young stepbrother, Prince Ravi, meaning 'sun'. Prince Ravi's mother, quite like the grievously misled Queen Kaikeyi of the Ramayana, wanted her son to be king. Although he was younger, she pressured her husband, the king, about it. In other words, she stalked off to the kopa griha or anger room, which every ancient Indian palace and grand mansion was equipped with. The anger room was the designated rage or sulk corner. When you were good and mad about something, you did not disturb the peace and order of the household by enacting nasty, vulgar scenes, not if you were high-born, at any rate. Instead, ancient Indian etiquette required that you retreat into the anger room to work it off and step out only when you had calmed down and were able to resume normal, polite behaviour. Or you waited in there, fuming, for whoever had upset you to knock on the door and apologize or talk it over. Whoever it was usually showed up very soon, for he or she knew their cues and duties equally well. This code of behaviour aimed at maximum damage control and not only preserved the tone of a good home but also kept the ruction under wraps, nicely frustrating the talebearers and those who relished the quarrels of others.

But unlike Raja Dasarath in the Ramayana, this king sternly said, 'No' to the improper and unjustified demands of his favourite queen. Fearing, however, for the safety of his elder sons, he told them to go live in the forest until he could send for them. Shocked but obedient, Prince Subhash, who was the Bodhisattva, and Prince Sashi, took off their fine muslin clothes, put away their golden armbands, anklets, earrings and chains, ate a last good dinner of cream of millet, curried pumpkin, spice-roasted blackbuck and stuffed peacocks, and lay down to sleep on their fine beds for one last night.

They were gone from the palace before daybreak, leaving the city unobserved, and made their way to the vast forest of sagaun or teak trees that lay beyond the River Ganga, carrying their swords, bows and arrows, a short axe, a set of fire stones and not much else.

Trailing them was their stepbrother, Prince Ravi, who had discovered what his mother had been up to in the anger room. Prince Ravi loved his brothers and was horribly embarrassed by his mother's unjust demand to make him king in place of his elder brother. He put away his own royal clothes, kitting himself out just like his brothers, and left the palace when they did, taking care to hide. When he caught up with them in the forest he fell at their feet humbly, made it clear that it was none of his doing, and insisted on going along.

Wandering north, the three princes reached the Himalayan foothills. They entered a lovely forest of shala trees (*Shorea robusta*, in case the matter teases) and spotted a lake shimmering through the trees. Prince Ravi, still somewhat on the back foot, besides being the youngest and obliged by good manners to wait on his elders, offered to fetch water for his brothers in lotus-leaf cups.

Thirsty and tired, the prince splashed into the lake's cool waters without looking around and exactly as it happened with the five Pandava brothers in the Mahabharata, the lake's resident yaksha spirit sprang out and caught him in its big, sharp claws.

'Answer my question or I won't let go of you,' it growled without preamble, but after all, yakshas were not known to be overly nice in these matters.

'Very well,' said the terrified prince.

'What is the teaching of the gods?' thundered the yaksha, and the prince quaked an answer at random, 'The sun and the moon,' which, of course, was the wrong answer. So the yaksha locked him away in a cave to be eaten later.

After some time, Prince Sashi came up to the lake, splashed in without a look and was promptly taken captive like Prince Ravi, except that his random and incorrect answer to the yaksha's question was, 'The four directions.' Into the yaksha's cave he went to join his brother.

Not long after, Prince Subhash made his way to the lake to look for his missing brothers. Being the smart prince—a fact his father recognized, which is why he had said, 'No,' sternly to his favourite queen—Prince Subhash looked around carefully and saw two sets of footprints going into the lake but none coming out. So he went around the lake with his sword drawn, looking for clues. The yaksha, which had been lying in wait behind a fat clump of lotuses and smacking its lips, looked him up and down and took his measure. Figuring out that this prince was not easy prey, the yaksha cannily disguised itself as a villager and accosted the prince politely with offers of food and drink.

'You must be the yaksha of this lake. What have you done with my brothers?' said the prince coldly. Shocked at being found out so quickly, the yaksha explained that it was empowered to eat any human being who went into the lake without knowing the right answer to the question, 'What is the teaching of the gods?'

'That's a very basic question,' snapped the prince, justly annoyed by the impertinence of it all.

'But you have to answer. Nobody got it right,' pouted the yaksha, miffed at being put in its place by a mere mortal.

'Good deeds bring glory. Bad deeds bring shame,' said the prince with the weary air of indulging a not very bright person.

'Hmpf. Clever, aren't we? So choose one brother,' said the wily yaksha, secretly delighted by this exchange, which was a refreshing break in the monotony of its easy life.

'Prince Ravi, of course, because he's my stepbrother and everyone will say we killed him otherwise,' said Prince Subhash.

Deeply pleased by this proof of common sense and self-preservation, the yaksha let Prince Subhash have both his brothers back and they all had nice baths and picnics and campfires with the yaksha telling the best and funniest stories, for he was really very well travelled and had accepted lake duty only as a retirement plan; until the day came when the royal messenger found the princes and took them home.

The meddlesome queen was dispatched on a long pilgrimage south across the Vindhya mountains and the king, as he had planned all along, swiftly had Prince Subhash installed as yuvraj or crown prince and put his kingdom on track.

6

The monk and the madhupayasa

A strongly cautionary Jataka tells of a jealous monk, a story that seems at first to be about workplace competition, if we can call this monk's situation that. Rather, we might wonder at the very concept of such monkery that encouraged able-bodied men to opt out of a productive working life and go on the dole. Such men, like the monk in this tale, had no reason to find a purpose to life beyond their bellies.

Xuan Zang, a seventh-century Chinese pilgrim to India, noted in his journal that, 'Among the products of the ground, rice and barley are most plentiful. With respect to edible herbs and plants, we may name ginger and mustard, melons and pumpkins and others. Onions and garlic are little known, and few people eat them . . . The most usual food is milk, butter, cream, soft sugar, sugar candy, the oil of the mustard seed, and all sorts of cakes made of grain.'

This may well have been the daily portion of the monk in this tale, who lived alone in a little village on the Upper Gangetic Plain. He was greatly enabled in his pleasant existence by a rich man of the village. Life was totally secure for this village monk with his belly always full. He lived in simple but cosy quarters and received only respect and courtesy from all. He slept as peacefully as a happy child and was entirely free to meditate, bathe and take long afternoon naps.

Into this idyll one morning came an older monk, of peaceful, learned ways. The village monk met him with due courtesy—giving him a welcome drink of buttermilk, offering his best spare robe, heating water for a bath and keeping out a brass cup of soap nut powder and oil for the visitor to rub on his body after the bath—all of which he was well-provided for by charity. Indeed, the village monk bustled about his preparations as proudly as any housewife to demonstrate the many comforts of his cottage.

After the bath, it was time to eat, which again was no problem. The village monk led the visiting monk to the rich man of the village, who promptly invited them to the midday meal. A feast was offered, to which both mendicants did full justice after chanting the customary blessing. After that, the visiting monk conversed knowledgeably and eloquently with his host on any number of subjects ranging from religious topics to insightful observations on the seasons and festivals, the subtle difficulties of chaturmaas—the four-month halt during the rains when travelling was forbidden— and news of the towns and villages visited along his travels. The rich man was charmed and took greatly to the visiting monk, showing him the utmost respect and hospitality and entreating him to come by every day for food and conversation.

That night, for the first time ever, the village monk was unable to sleep. The worm of jealousy had entered his head and writhed about so much that it kept him wide awake. Burnt up by his night of misery, the village monk did not wake his visitor for the round of morning alms. The Jataka says that he scratched so softly with his nail on the visiting monk's door that not even a mouse could have heard him. After this paltry start to the day, he could scarcely mask his animosity and snubbed his visitor at every opportunity.

The visiting monk, though hurt by such bad behaviour, understood the agony that the village monk was going through and pitied him deeply. He meditated all morning until he reached a higher level of inner peace.

Later that day, the village monk went to call on the rich man, who asked after the visiting monk. The village monk glibly said that he had knocked on the visitor's door but had heard no answer. The rich man then filled the village monk's begging bowl with delicious madhupayasa made of rice, milk, ghee, sugar and honey. After the monk had eaten, the rich man took away the bowl, washed it in scented water and refilled it to be taken back to the visiting monk.

Unwilling to share, the village monk wondered frantically how best to dispose of the evidence. After some searching, he noticed a field that had just been burnt by farmers to make the soil better. It glowed with live coals, on which the village monk poured out the payasa to the last drop. It went hissing up in smoke, leaving a miasma of burnt milk.

When he got back home, he found that the visiting monk had gone away. The Jataka says it took the village monk 1001 lives after that to recover his peace of mind, which had burnt up along with the madhupayasa. It's likely that the outrage of wasting the work of others also had its karmic consequences.

7

The bowman's strategy

This somewhat peculiar Jataka seems to illustrate how even very bright people can suffer from low self-esteem and, instead of taking their chances fair and square, can resort to cunning in order to get ahead. In effect, it seems to say that some folks try to get away with fooling people all the time because they've already made up their minds that they don't stand a chance otherwise.

Anyhow, once upon a time when Brahmadatta was king of Varanasi, a son was born to a poor priest in a village in the Upper Gangetic Plain. The boy was born a midget with a crooked body, which made the neighbours shake their heads

9

39

and remember the sage Ashtavakra—or 'Eight Twists' of epic fame, who was similarly crooked of frame since birth.

However, the priest, helped by almost everybody in the village and from the villages nearby, scraped up the cart fare to send his son to a first-class guru in Varanasi for an education. There, the boy fell in with princes of the northern kingdoms, and because he was possessed of utter and absolute dignity and spoke pleasantly even to those who tried to tease him, he obtained the respect and favour of everyone around.

Thanks to the company of the princes, he learnt to be an expert archer in addition to his book learning. When their formal education was over, it was time to go home or go out and earn a living. The princes rode off to their father's kingdoms with breezy invitations to visit but the poor priest's son knew that he could not go home empty-handed and had to make his own way in the world.

Leaving Varanasi, he travelled south in search of employment to a big city in the rich Andhra country. The people of this region were very well set up and good-looking and went about with a bright, confident air. The women wore flowers in their hair and proudly held up their heads. The language was different and so was the food. The broad tree-lined streets on which the royal elephants walked in procession were very different from the cosy, narrow lanes of Varanasi.

Out in this big world and away from the cocoon of the gurukul, the bright little bowman completely lost his nerve. He forgot that he was skilled and learned and had managed to live on good terms with the world. His confidence slipped away and his tejas or inner lustre, which shone thanks to the good company he had kept and the goodwill of those at home, began to fade. He lost sight of his kritagyata or obligation to the well-wishers who had brought him this far and thought, 'If I show up before the king, he is sure to ask what a dwarf like me is good for,' and came up with a cunning plan instead: 'Why should I not ask a bigger man to be my work partner and earn my living behind his grander presence?'

The little bowman approached a mountainous weaver called Bhimasena. Without ever having put in a single job application to test his defeatist theory, the little bowman mourned to the weaver that nobody wanted a midget, even if he was a brilliant archer. He suggested that the man-mountain should pretend to be an archer himself and seek employment with the king and pass off the real bowman, his secret field officer, as his page.

The faux archer was hired on the spot along with his page. But soon, work appeared. A tiger had left the cover of the jungle and was on the prowl in the surrounding countryside. Plump goats and calves were disappearing from farms at an alarming rate and the tiger required urgent dispatch. The affected praja came in a body to petition the king to do something about it at once. As a matter of course, the king and some of his best huntsmen would have personally tracked and killed the tiger to renew the confidence and affection of the public. Besides, they would have had a day's excellent sport. That was the royal way in ancient India.

But the king and his ministers were up to their eyeballs just then in working out a complicated river treaty with the neighbouring kingdom and had no time to be chasing tigers. The king bethought himself of his new employee and ordered him to take care of the business.

The weaver rushed home to the little bowman, who thought it over carefully. His considered advice was this: 'Muster a strong band of country folk to march to the spot with at least 100 bowmen. When you know that the tiger is near, you bolt into the thicket and lie flat on your face. The country folk will be so worked up by then that they will beat the tiger to death; and as soon as he is quite dead, you bite off a creeper with your teeth and draw near, trailing the creeper. At the sight of the dead tiger, you will burst out with: "Who killed the tiger? I meant to lead it like an ox to the king and had just stepped into the thicket to find a creeper." Then the country folk will be very frightened and bribe you heavily not to report them to the king. You will be credited with slaying the tiger and the king too will give you lots of money.'

And that is exactly what happened.

Did the man-mountain bother sharing the booty with the little bowman whom he could have squashed flat with one thump? Why did the little bowman not go along and shoot the tiger to prove himself when he had the chance? Why did he cheat the king instead and contrive to make the public do the dirty work and on top of that, trick them out of their money? Why, when he had so many blessings to count, did he let his inner self, which was straight and true, get as twisted as his body?

We must assume that the original audience of this tale understood the subtle message in it and was not disposed instead to literally view those born with twisted limbs and dwarfism or dysplasia tarda with suspicion. What a complicated story, to be sure, but we are free to make full allowance for the Indian penchant for coded messages.

8

Haridatt and the serpent

Snakes and serpents have a bad name in Semitic mythology because in that story the devil in the guise of a serpent tempted Eve to eat the forbidden apple, though it was scarcely the serpents' fault that their form came in handy for lurking about in trees.

Out East, snakes and serpents get a lot of respect in Indian mythology as wise and powerful beings who serve the biggest gods. They are held to be affectionate and generous and generally supportive of human beings, but also need to be tiptoed around carefully because they can be moody and sensitive. They are also said to be the most finicky about polite behaviour. In the old days, it was considered very good training in the ways of the world to be taught how to address snakes properly in their shrines.

The way a Jataka tells it, a poor farmer named Haridatt lay down one day for an afternoon nap in the shade of a tree by his field. When he woke up, he happened to see a serpent gliding out of an anthill nearby. Saluting the snake as the naag devta, or the snake godling who guarded his fields from rats and mice, he left a bowl of milk for it before he went home. The next day, he was astonished to find a gold coin in the bowl. This became a pattern and prevailed for many days. Haridatt grew very prosperous and built himself a fine new homestead with rafters of the best teak, and big, new barns and sheds. He bought the adjoining fields off his neighbours, dug a new well and had water channels made, and naturally, being an Indian farmer, bought a whole herd of the finest milch cows and two big, strong buffaloes at the cattle fair to turn the wheel of a grand new oil press he had made for the village.

He began to take an interest in pilgrimage and donated freely to the post-monsoon renovation of the local temple and on his own initiative, he had a fine dharamshala or rest house made for travellers. He put on a clever charade to explain his growing prosperity, going off one day on his own to a big town in the region. When he came back, he spread a wholly imaginary tale about being blessed by an itinerant holy man and being led in a dream to a cache of gold under a big pipal tree that stood well away from the king's highway.

The villagers bought the story. They began to look up to Haridatt and it was not long before he was made the village headman; and he looked very fine at meetings, twirling his big moustache and laying down the law in local disputes. When the local feudal lord up in his fort got his son married, Haridatt was invited to the wedding feast after the bride was brought home. He took along a silken pouch of gold coins as a present. More importantly, whenever the king's revenue officer came to collect tax from the village, he stayed at Haridatt's house and told anyone who cared to listen that there was no better host than Haridatt within a radius of a thousand kos.

Through all this, Haridatt never missed a morning at the anthill if he was at home and never failed to fervently thank the snake each time.

Haridatt had not told a soul about the snake and the gold coins. Even his wife fell for the absurd story of the dream and the pipal tree, and his children were too young to ask questions for the first few years of this miraculous spell of good fortune. By the time they were older, they were so used to prosperity that they never thought to ask how their father had made his money.

Haridatt was now so well set up that there was not a single comfort lacking in his life. He was healthy, wealthy and extremely happy. He had enough to feed, house, clothe and marry off the next three generations of his family. He had taken to wearing a solid gold bracelet with a snake etched on it that he drolly referred to as his lucky charm. Even the village priest, normally the single window for such magicking, was content to smile indulgently.

However, one time, when Haridatt needed to travel to the next town for a couple of days, he found that he grudged having to miss even one day's yield of gold coin. He had never minded before, since the snake's excellent manners made it repay every offering, but this time he minded very much. Why should he lose a single one of those gold coins just because he needed to be away?

Without going into the details, he told his son to take a bowl of milk to the snake that lived in the anthill. The next morning, when the son saw the gold coin, he thought, 'There must be so many gold coins under this spot. I will kill the snake tomorrow with my stick and take them all.' The next day he waited until the snake emerged to drink the milk and aimed a blow at its head with his stout bamboo lathi.

The serpent (did I mention that it was a splendid king cobra?) recoiled in pain and bit the young man, who died writhing in agony right there. The villagers found him and promptly cremated him, for that was the custom.

When Haridatt came home to this horrible news, he grieved bitterly for his son. But so deep was his addiction to the gold coins that he went back as usual to the anthill with a bowl of milk and praised the snake as his benefactor.

The snake poked its head out and surveyed him with contempt. 'I despise your greed,' it said. 'Your son struck my head and I bit him in rage. How can I forget the blow, or you, his death?'

Scrupulously correct to the end, it let fall a rare pearl as a parting gift and vanished forever.

9

Two otters and an expectedly wily jackal

The moral of this Jataka is well known in modern Hindi as bandar-baant, meaning 'the monkey's division' of goods where, in a fight between two parties, the monkey, as the arbitrator, leaves them with very little and takes away the most for itself.

A variation in this theme is found in a tale told by the Sakyamuni to the assembly of monks during a retreat at the Jetavana monastery. Jetavana or 'Jeta's Forest' was next to the city of Shravasti, which was one of the six great cities of the Upper Gangetic Plain during the Buddha's time.

The Buddha spent nineteen of the forty-five annual retreats that he conducted in his lifetime at Jetavana and this Jataka is one of the teaching stories that he told the monks as a caution against letting outsiders take advantage of in-house quarrels or disagreements. How very pleasant it must have been for the rows and rows of saffron-clad monks to sit listening quietly in the cool, dark shade of those ancient mango trees, to a story told by the Sakyamuni himself, in his low, clear voice, with its humorous inflections and steady thread of common sense.

Long ago, says the Jataka, when Brahmadatta was king of Varanasi, there lived a jackal named Mayavi—an apt name, meaning 'illusionist' or 'deceiver'. The jackal found himself a mate and they lived happily by the River Varuna, or perhaps it was the Assi, both of which are minor tributaries of the great Ganga that combine to give Varanasi its name. Well, one day, Mrs Mayavi told her husband that she longed to eat fresh river fish. Happy to oblige, the jackal went scouting by the riverbank, hoping to steal something from a fishwife's basket, when he suddenly saw a most interesting sight.

Two sleek, handsome otters were out by the river in search of lunch. One of them spotted a fine big fish and leapt into the water after it, but the fish was strong and helped by the current, it almost got away. 'Help me!' called the otter in the water and its friend on the bank jumped in at once and, between them, they landed their catch.

Then, despite rejoicing in fine classical names like Gambhir meaning 'thoughtful', 'influential' and 'considerate', and Anuthi meaning 'unique' and 'extraordinary', the two otters fell into a squabble about how to share their lunch, though they argued very politely.

'You caught this, so please do the sharing,' said Anuthi first, with a deep namaste.

'Not without your help, so you must do the honours,' bowed Gambhir, with exquisite courtesy.

Neither party would budge from its stand. And so it went on for a good half hour, driven by silly pride about which of the two was the more mannerly while the fine big fish lay patiently between them waiting to be eaten. The jackal had hidden himself behind a big tree at some distance from the bank and watched these proceedings with keen interest.

When the two otters, worn out with arguing, flopped down on either side of their catch, the jackal judged it the right moment to step out and greeted them very civilly.

'Welcome, friend,' said the exhausted otters. 'Perhaps you can settle our dispute for us.'

'Why, certainly,' grinned the jackal. 'Here's how.'

And very swiftly, he bit the fish into three portions with his sharp teeth.

'Here's the head, for you,' he said, pushing it at Gambhir. 'And here's the tail, for you,' and pushed that at Anuthi. 'And here's my share, for settling your dispute.'

And in the blink of an eye, he seized the entire fat midsection of the fish and bounded up the riverbank and home to his delighted wife.

'But you can't swim. How did you get this?' she marvelled between bites.

'Serves them right for fighting,' said Mayavi, thinking of the two silly otters.

10

The baby quail and the forest fire

A certain Jataka goes that the Bodhisattva was once born as a baby quail in a forest in ancient Magadha, which lies on the eastern side of north India. Of course, the baby quail's parents knew nothing of their region's history or that it was a holy land where saints and sages had walked and taught. They had made their nest in a fine old lodhra tree (a *Symplocos racemosa*) of which entire forests grew in ancient Magadha, as noted with enthusiasm in several old texts.

Physicians and their apprentices made regular forays into the forests of Magadha to gather precious lodhra bark for a whole range of

Ayurvedic medicine, for this bark was cherished then, and is still cherished, as divya aushadi or divine medicine. However, the little quail family was undisturbed. Their tree grew so deep in the forest that it was too hidden for even the boldest elephant-hunter or honey-gatherer to discover. The baby quail's parents flew out every day to forage for food for their nestling, and life was nicely on course and proceeding exactly as it ought.

However, a sudden forest fire broke out one day during the height of summer as the rains had failed the previous year. The birds and animals fled in terror as the fire tore unstoppably through the forest. As terrified as the rest, the baby quail's parents completely lost awareness of everything but the need to save their own lives and flew away, leaving their baby behind.

Hearing the terrible noise of crackling flames, falling branches and the cries of stampeding forest creatures, the baby quail stretched its tiny body to peep out of its nest. When it saw the fire advancing purposefully, it understood the situation at once. 'My poor parents have fled in fear, abandoning me to my fate,' it thought. 'If my wings were grown, I would fly. If I had legs, I could try to run away. But I can do neither and so I must die.'

At that moment of cold clarity in the burning heat, the baby quail found inspiration.

'There are only two real powers in this world,' it found itself thinking, despite its dreadful situation or perhaps because of it. 'They are the might of truth and the might of goodness. I completely understand and accept the truth that I am weak and I am alone. But I also know that there must be so much goodness stored in the world, so much merit accumulated by the good deeds of good people in the past and even now, in the living present. Let me call upon both forces.'

Making the most enormous mental effort to block out its terror, the baby quail began to switch off its sight, hearing and other senses, and to concentrate its thoughts into total stillness. When it had withdrawn deep into its head and could neither hear the noise outside nor feel the heat, it said, 'Here I am alone, with wings that cannot fly. By this truth and by the faith that I find in me, I ask you, O Fire, to please turn back without harming me or the others.'

And, says the Jataka, the fire retreated sixteen lengths and died out because of the baby quail's satyakriya or act of truth.

11

Samyukta and the robbers

A Shan Buddhist story from Myanmar shows us how Buddhist missionaries used local stories to convey the message that it was generally better to manage life's little situations with maximum diplomacy and minimum damage.

The Shan Plateau to the eastern side of Myanmar was a rich and pleasant land, inhabited by people of mostly nine Asian backgrounds, such as the Mongol, Chin, Kachin and Kayah, to name a few. Shan people include the Tai Ahom in India's northeastern state of Assam, where they are said to have ruled for almost 600 years. Gold and silver were mined in the Shan Plateau and also Burmese

61

rubies, the best in the world. Large lakes, rushing rivers and vast limestone caves carved with over 6000 images of the Buddha made the countryside beautiful, as did tall forests of teak, thousands of lush rice fields and the most delicious fruit and vegetables—the gifts of good climate, rich soil and hard work.

Long ago, in this former earthly paradise, there lived a rich landlord called Savatika in the village of Kokkalu, who rejoiced in the absolute and undisputed ownership of many buffaloes, much pastureland and rooms full of silver and gold. He was a mahaarthika, an old Sanskrit term of honour for someone who was rich and powerful.

Savatika was the patron of the able-bodied young men of Kokkalu village, who were both soldiers and farmers. They trained in warfare and weaponry and had regular games of strength and rigorous exercise and drill to keep themselves fit for fighting and ready for raiders. In between, they farmed their rich land, went to the temple and ate enormous meals of pork, chicken, fish, fresh greens and rice, after which they chewed quantities of betel leaf and sometimes smoked a roll-up of tobacco. Harvest moons awoke their wit, and religious festivals like Buddha Purnima, their piety.

News came one day that the Buddha himself was to visit a nearby place in the course of his travels. This was such electrifying news that everyone wanted to go. All the able-bodied young men of Kokkalu planned to go together on the appointed day to seek the Buddha's blessings.

Hearing of this expedition, a local bandit king was quick to realize that Kokkalu would be left virtually unguarded. He had long had a wistful eye on Savatika's wealth and decided that this was an excellent opportunity to raid and loot the mahaarthika. However, Savatika heard of it through the jungle telegraph some time after the able-bodied young men had set off, and began to hastily arm the few men left in the village with bows and arrows, to mount whatever defence they could.

But Savatika's little daughter, Samyukta, came up with another plan. She persuaded her father to deflect the robbers with finesse instead of fighting. This was pleasing to a man of property on several counts for it did away with the need for direct conflict, which reduced the risk to life and to the farm, the homestead and the livestock. Savatika agreed, but since he was also a father, he quietly slipped Samyukta his little jade-handled dagger for he had watched her slaughter chickens for lunch with a steady arm and was assured that she would not lose her nerve in case matters turned difficult.

Tying up their long black hair with their prettiest ribbons and gathering their water jars, Samyukta and her little troop of friends walked innocently to the edge of the mango grove, where the desperate ruffians had stopped to rest before launching their attack. The robbers were charmed to see the sweet little girls who spoke to them as if they were respectable people, and were won over by Samyukta's friendly ways and polite words. The bandit king was very pleased when Samyukta offered to fetch them lunch.

The girls came back to the bandits as planned with four wheelbarrows bearing rice, fish, onions, pumpkins and salt. Nor had they forgotten tea and tobacco. While they handed out these luxuries with more sweet words, a prearranged drum roll from the village went 'da-da-da-drrr-r-r-r'. When the bandits leapt up in fright, the little maidens fibbed that it was only the sepoys left behind to protect the village during the absence of the other men. The bandit king rapidly reconsidered his plans and the entire band melted into the jungle, barely stopping to snatch up the provisions.

The able-bodied young men came back to Kokkalu after having offered their respects to the Buddha, which had filled them with good, peaceful thoughts. However, they were furious when they heard about the intended attack and were all for a counter-raid on the robbers' jungle hideout. But Savatika calmed them down by pointing out that the bandits had been sent away without violence. He invited the young men to a big feast instead and so they sat down in great good humour and made a big fuss of their little sisters, and especially of Samyukta, for managing it all so well, while the bandits, who were now far away, swore among themselves never to go near Kokkalu village again.

12

Pingala, the public woman

The haunting case of Pingala, the public woman, may be found in one of India's favourite books, the *Srimad Bhagvatam*, that is cherished even today as the biography of Sri Krishna.

In the portion concerning Pingala in the *Srimad Bhagvatam*, Krishna's ancestor King Yadu happened to meet a young priest whose face and manners shone with serene self-possession.

King Yadu was so impressed by the priest's air of nobility and wisdom that he wanted to know how the priest had achieved it. With becoming humility, the priest said that he had had many teachers including an ajgar or serpent and the pancha bhuta, the Five Elements of earth, water, air, fire and ether. He explained what he had observed and learnt from each.

And then, he shocked King Yadu, saying, 'In the city of Videha, there used to be a public woman called Pingala. Now hear, O King, what I learnt from her.'

'I can readily accept that the natural world and its creatures have many lessons for us. But really, a public woman . . . I don't see how . . .' murmured the king, not wishing to seem ill-mannered but unable to hide how startled he was.

The young priest smiled and got on with his story:

Pingala stood at her doorway as usual one evening, displaying her beautiful form to attract passing customers. Her city, Videha, was the proud capital of the kingdom of Mithila on the eastern side of north India. Mithila had a very good opinion of itself as a famous seat of learning and as the holy land of many spiritually revelatory dramas played out between old lawgivers and kings.

Above all, it was proud that Sita, also called
Maithili, Princess of Mithila, was renowned
in the Indic world as the heroine of the grand
Sanskrit epic, the Ramayana. Ever after her
story had become known to all, every Hindu
bride was handed over to her bridegroom by
her father, or whoever stood in for her father
at the wedding, with the very words said by
Maithili's father, King Janaka, at her wedding,
'*Iyam Sita, mama suta* . . .' (This is Sita, my
daughter.)

Pingala often thought about Princess
Maithili, or Vaidehi as she was also called,
and of her curious fate, which was to be
punished and exiled by her husband, the king
of Ayodhya, for no fault of hers. A bad person
had kidnapped Sita and her husband had
fought to rescue her and had even made her go
through trial by fire to satisfy the vulgar public
curiosity about her 'purity'. But once tarnished,
a woman's reputation was not easily recovered
in old societies. When a washerman in Ayodhya
had quarrelled with his wife and said she was

'as shameless as Sita for living in another man's house', the king of Ayodhya had cast out his queen as a blot on the throne, and had banished her to the jungle to fend for herself, not even caring that she was then pregnant.

Through it all, the heartbroken princess had been staunchness personified and no person, man or woman, could think of her without feeling wretched at the injustice of it and wanting to cry. What an inhuman standard it seemed to hold up for a human woman, especially for a victim of circumstance. Be that as it may, the public took her fate very personally and to star Sita's name in their own weddings was their way of trying to make it up to her memory.

Pingala herself had been born into a respectable family and been taught her prayers and told many stories from the scriptures. But her parents had died of an illness and there was no one left to care for her. She had been put to work as a maid in a merchant's kitchen and was seduced by the son of the house.

Pingala, the public woman

Thrown out on the street when discovered, Pingala had no reputation left and nowhere to go. Videha's richest bawd had picked her up and taught her the tricks of the trade. Pingala had done reasonably well for herself. She had a little house of her own now in the quarter of the public women and could afford to employ a maid to cook and clean while she devoted herself to looking her best with scented baths, regular oil massages, sandalwood face packs and carefully chosen clothes and ornaments.

But Pingala was very lonely and longed for a secure life. She fantasized every day about that one rich man who would fall in love with her and look after her for good with affection and respect. She prayed every day for this wish to be granted and worried about it all the time. She worried about it that evening, in the soft purple twilight of Videha as she stood at her door, and worried about it when she looked up, as she always did, at the evening star, and went on worrying till midnight, when suddenly she had a startling revelation.

'Just what am I doing making myself so unhappy, selling myself to men who are lamentable themselves, desperately hoping that someone will love me and look after me? Am I so unintelligent that I can't see how pointless this is? The best way to be happy is to be unafraid and live my life confidently with the faith that I'll cope, that "someone" is with me already,' she found herself thinking, amazed at her own clarity of thought. 'Nor need I be ashamed of the life I was forced to live. After all, I belong to Videha, which means "bodiless". My new understanding of what life is really about has set me free of my body.'

With that resolve, Pingala shut the door and sat down on her bed. Serene in her newfound realization, she went to sleep happy.

'And so I learnt from Pingala that people can always remake their lives with independent reasoning,' said the young priest to the fascinated King Yadu.

13

'Tell me your father's name'

Long ago in the forest-covered plains of western Kuru–Panchala, the region now known as Delhi–Haryana–western Uttar Pradesh, where the then-queenly Yamuna flowed, somebody put together a book of lectures, stories and conversations in Sanskrit on the nature of the world and the proper goals of mankind. This particular book was the grand old *Chandogya Upanishad.*

They say it was the sage Uddalaka Aruni who compiled it back in BCE in eight chapters. Its core idea is the 'oneness of the One', meaning that the supreme soul or life force, is in everything, in every direction. The most famous words in the *Chandogya*

Upanishad are '*tat tvam asi*' meaning 'thou art That'. This cryptic remark is understood as saying, 'Since everything in the world is interconnected, who do you think you are if not part of it all?'

Notably, this Upanishad says that life is a celebration; a rather wonderful party, and the presents we bring to it are ethical behaviour, goodwill to all and the habit of speaking the truth. Glum and harsh behaviour is not the correct way to repay prana, the life breath, thanks to which we're guests at the party of life.

Just as notably the *Chandogya Upanishad* makes it clear that a brahmin is the highest class of human being, but it's got nothing to do with birth and everything to do with being honest and truthful and, therefore, of spotless character and fit to guide society. Not otherwise. So the Upanishad sets a high standard for people as people and not because of their ancestry, and tells us what became of a likely lad in a small settlement in western Kuru–Panchala.

His mother, Jabala, was a single parent who worked for a living as a maid in several people's houses. The little boy went with her wherever she did and observed all kinds of people in all kinds of homes. His mother had taught him not to touch anything that did not belong to him and not ask for anything in another's house. The boy never gave trouble and nobody minded him trailing behind his mother. He was a shy, silent child, who had to be coaxed to talk and said 'thank you' solemnly if somebody gave him a stick of sugar candy or a little clay toy to pull on a string.

When he was about eight years old, his mother took on a new job, helping the local priest's wife clean and wash her courtyard every day. The boy was no stranger to the sound of Sanskrit chants in the settlement, which seemed to him a very wonderful thing full of power and mystery. The hard-edged consonants rang in his ears with a deeply satisfying sound and he longed to know what they meant, and to address the splendid gods himself on behalf of all in those mysterious, beautiful words and meters. He learnt to recognize the rhythms of the chants, and the priest's son with whom he went bird-nesting and swimming and played hide-and-seek in the mango groves told him the names of the meters in play, which delighted the boy. At last he had a real piece of knowledge from that world.

'The *Gayatri* meter has twenty-four syllables. The *Trishtup* has forty-four. The *Jagati* has forty-eight,' he would murmur, dying to know more. One day, the priest's son told him the first line of the Rig Veda, the very first line of poetry known to the world.

The boy slipped off to the banks of the Yamuna, feeling instinctively that fire needed to be balanced with water. '*Agnim-īle purohitaṃ yajñasya devaṃ ṛtvījam,*' he crooned in ecstasy to himself, 'I praise Ignis, the chosen one, the priest, god and performer of sacrifice.' The river gurgled in encouragement but that was the sweet-natured Yamuna for you, ever sympathetic to those who approached her with a secret or in trouble of some kind.

'I want to study. I want to go to school,' he told the river and raced home before his mother could worry.

There were visitors next week at the priest's, students on their way to join the gurukul of a sage who lived some distance away, Rishi Haridrumata Gautama.

'What a mouthful!' laughed the new students in a spasm of, 'May we be children for two minutes more?' before they went off to school to grow up.

The boy felt his heart beating fast. He must go with them. He followed them all the way to the gurukul and saw that Rishi Gautama had a strong, sensible sort of face and the Guru Ma, his wife, smiled kindly in welcome at the new boys.

He waited for his turn to speak to the guru.

'Sir, please may I learn with the others?' he said.

The teacher smiled. 'Of course, you may, if your parents permit it. Tell me your father's name, my boy.'

The boy was dumbstruck. His father! He did not know who his father was. His mother had never once mentioned his father and he had never thought to ask.

'Sir, I'll be back soon with the answer,' he said desperately and turned to leave.

When he got home, the boy ran to his mother and said, 'Mother, who was my father? They're asking at school before they'll admit me.'

'Do you want to leave me, child, and go away to gurukul?' said his mother, with a sudden catch in her voice. She could not bear to think of her little boy leaving home.

'I don't want to leave you, Mother. But I must go to school. I cannot sleep thinking of it, sometimes. The rishi's school is not far, Mother. Please will you let me go?' said the boy yearningly.

His mother looked at his desperate face and her heart melted.

'You have my permission to go,' she said softly. She went to the back of their hut and rummaged around, looking for something.

The boy waited patiently, not daring to say a word in case she changed her mind.

'Take this for your teacher's wife. You cannot go empty-handed to a guru, it is the custom to take a present,' said his mother, coming back with a clean cotton sari that the village priest's wife had given her.

The boy took it eagerly, but suddenly his face fell. 'Mother,' he said, 'Thank you so much for this. But I also need to know the name of my father.'

His mother sat down and looked at him steadily.

'Listen carefully, my son. You have nothing to be ashamed of if you always tell the truth, however difficult or embarrassing it may seem. The truth about us is that I am an orphan and was sent to work as a maid when I was a little girl. I worked as a maid in many places. Not only did I have to do all the work, I had to personally look after all the guests. Sometimes this meant I had to sleep with them. I had to sleep with many men, my son. And then I had you and decided to go away and work only where I had a chance of bringing you up without having to do that. This village has been our haven since you were a baby.'

'Mother! But who was my father, then?' exclaimed the boy.

'I have no clue about your father, my son. My name is Jabala. Your name is Satyakama. So tell

79

them at school that you're Satyakama Jabali, the son of Jabala.'

The boy looked at his mother in silence while he tried to properly understand what she had just told him and she looked lovingly back at him. He smiled suddenly, a joyous, carefree smile and touched his mother's feet. He hugged her hard and rushed back to the gurukul, clutching the present she had given him for his teacher's wife.

He went up to the guru, saluted him deeply and repeated exactly what his mother had said. He felt neither fear nor shame for his heart overflowed with love and respect for his brave mother. Let the guru reject him, he would look for another teacher or another or another . . .

But instead, the guru looked hard at him and then leapt up, beaming. He hugged the boy and said, 'My child, well are you named Satyakama, the one who loves truth. Such a one as you is a true "brahmin", who is meant to serve society. A "brahmin" upholds an ideal by his thoughts and behaviour. Anyone of exemplary character is a "brahmin", it is an ideal, not an accident of birth.

It is a mistake to assume otherwise. A "respectable" or "high" birth is of no consequence in this matter, Satyakama. Your mother has brought you up well and given you the best foundation for your nature and character—the fearless love of truth. I salute her. You shall learn everything I can teach you.'

'And nothing was omitted in the teaching,' says the Upanishad with satisfaction. 'Nothing was omitted.'

14

The boy who was sold

This nasty but moving story that many people don't get to hear for reasons you'll soon notice, is from the *Aitareya Brahmana* section of the Rig Veda. It goes back to early antiquity, to the fabled times of no less than 'good King Harishchandra' of Ayodhya, to when the gods are thought to have walked openly among mortals.

The story goes that King Harishchandra married many wives and had the usual problem: there was no son to inherit the kingdom. He went for counselling to Devrishi Narada, who advised Harishchandra to pray to the ancient god, Varuna. Varuna did grant him his wish but the king came out having made a dreadful bargain—a life for a life. Harishchandra would get his son but at some point, he would have to offer a human life in exchange to Varuna. Perhaps the god was testing him, in which case Harishchandra had spectacularly failed.

Soon enough, Prince Rohitasva (Sanskrit for 'red horse') was born to gladden Raja Harishchandra's heart and the old bargain was conveniently forgotten. But when Rohitasva grew up, Varuna testily reminded the king of his promise just to see him run around; for under his virtuous manner, Harishchandra was guilty of vanity, the 'I'm such a decent person' kind that the gods find particularly irritating. When the king nervously explained the matter to his rather spoilt son, Rohitasva rushed off to the forest to find a man to sacrifice to Varuna. Of course, nobody agreed to be offered up since human sacrifice was not the custom. Rohitasva began to be afraid that Varuna would want to drag him off instead. He wandered around for nearly six years looking for a sacrificial victim and his fond father Harishchandra literally suffered agonies while he was away, for Varuna was not amused by these delaying tactics and inflicted the most hideous stomach ache on Harishchandra as a fine for defaulting.

At last, Rohitasva stumbled across Ajigarta, a priest whose belly ached from another kind of punishment: hunger. Ajigarta, for all his grand bloodline from the important old sage Angiras, had been kicked out of his settlement for malpractice. Nobody would give him work after that and he had turned into a Vedic hillbilly, eking out a precarious existence in the woods with his wife and three sons, Shunapuchha (dogtail), Shunashepa (dogdick) and Shunalangula (dogbutt). Their names reflected Ajigarta's warped sense of humour. Ajigarta offered Rohitasva one of his sons for a hundred cows, which would set him up nicely. However, he said he would not part with his eldest son, whom he loved the best. Ajigarta's wife set up a squall at once that she would not part with her youngest son, her baby.

'My parents don't love me at all,' thought Shunashepa, the middle son, deeply shocked.

'What's the point of hanging on to life if nobody loves me, not even my mother?'

He stepped forward, his face burning with the shame of it. 'You may have me as your sacrifice, Prince,' he said politely and turned his face away from his family.

Rohitasva took Shunashepa at once to the palace and Harishchandra decided to combine his sacrifice with the Rajasuya ceremony, which was his own anointment as 'King of kings'. Four of the greatest sages of the age were to conduct the sacrifice: Vishwamitra as the hotr (the leader or conductor of the sacrifice), Jamadagni as the adhvaryu (the doer or manager of the fire and the offerings, especially the soma juice so pleasing to gods and men), Ayasya as the udgatr (the chanter of hymns from the Sama Veda) and Vasishta as the brahmana (the chanter of hymns from the Atharva Veda). But all four holy men refused to bind Shunashepa to the sacrificial stake and Rohitasva had to bribe Ajigarta, who had trailed along to see the fun, with another hundred cows to do it. Meanwhile, Shunashepa tried to process two devastating things together:

his father's participation in his sacrifice and the fact that he would soon be killed.

At the appointed hour, when the altars had been built in strict accordance with sacred geometry, Shunashepa was led to the sacrificial stake and bound firmly to it by his own father. The dreadful moment had arrived, reflected in the grim, set faces of the priests. Ajigarta had tied the cords with deadly efficiency around his son's thin body, and the rope bit into his skin. The terrible silence was punctured only by the hiss and crackle of flames in the fire pit, where offerings would be poured, the lowing of a cow in the distance, the clink of an ugrani ladle on a panchapatra beaker; each small sound magnified to frightening loudness in that quiet.

The preliminary chants began, the magic meters twisting through the air to unravel the minds of the hearers and restring them into one luminous sutra that would carry the heat of the sacred fire to the gods.

Then, as the king reached for the sharp blade with which to slit his throat, the force of feeling that consumes the unloved shook Shunashepa. Secretly coached in his one chance to live by the leader of the sacrifice, Vishwamitra, whose name meant 'friend of all the world', Shunashepa looked heavenwards. Slokas poured from his throat, verses of unearthly beauty praising Varuna whose sacrifice he was. It was as though he was gathering all the love that was denied him and offering it to the god as a parting gesture, a graceful act of generosity from someone who was helpless and possessed of nothing but his soul as a human being.

The assembled rishis, rajas and praja sat stone still. Nobody could move or speak in the spell of that confident sound. Slowly, so slowly that it went unnoticed at first, the cords binding Shunashepa loosened and slid to the ground. Shunashepa had pulled the god's head down by the ear with his grace under pressure; he had uncurled Varuna's tight fist into an open palm.

*

After this incredible event, Shunashepa was adopted by Vishwamitra and soon became a scholar of note, driven by his need to escape his unhappy past and determined to make something of himself unlike his father. He cut his emotional losses and had no more truck with his parents whose 'love' had been exposed as hollow and not worth having; and, as he soon discovered, he was all the better for it.

15

The canal on the Kaveri

If this story has a moral or an inspiration, it is probably this: that truth can actually prove stranger than fiction and, therefore, once in an extraordinary while if nobody is hurt, the motive is pure and the cause is worthy and not for personal gain, it may be all right to suspend disbelief and go with the flow. This was the case at any rate in 1804 when the British rebuilt the Grand Anicut on the River Kaveri in the southeast of the Indian subcontinent.

The Grand Anicut—derived from anai kattu in Tamil meaning a 'holding structure', like a canal or dam—was made by King Karikala Chola in the early centuries of the first millennium. It is one of the world's most ancient canals to still be in use and Karikala, whose legends are many, is praised in several poetic works from the Sangam or Academy Era of Tamil literature between the second and fourth centuries CE.

The backstory to this feat is that the rice farmers of the Tamil country in the Kaveri Delta had a complex irrigation system for their paddy fields. They were a hard-working lot who managed to grow three rice crops a year, which nobody else in south India could do in those days. However, these farmers had a problem. They petitioned King Karikala to figure out a way to regulate the monsoon floodwaters between the rivers Kaveri and Kollidam. Much of the Kaveri's waters were carried off by the Kollidam, which ran in a lower bed. So King Karikala had a kallanai or stone canal made across the Kaveri's outlet into the Kollidam. Gigantic boulders were laid across the riverbed like a long snake by Karikala's corvée, which possibly included his prisoners of war. A grand canal was made that was 1008 feet long, 40 to 60 feet wide and 15 to18 feet high; the biggest work made for the public good anywhere in India until the British engineers arrived.

Between 1804 and 1806, the British made some repairs and added sluice gates and an overhead bridge to Karikala's canal. After a huge effort of many months, when at last the water gates were raised, an inspection officer found that the nineteenth span of the bridge on the Kollidam side had collapsed overnight. It was rebuilt with greater care over the next month but promptly collapsed again. They remade it for the third time with super-close supervision, but no, boom! All of a sudden, it fell down again as a mass of stone and rubble. The stupefied engineers wondered what on earth was going on.

A strange story came out in the agitated discussions that followed these catastrophes. The construction inspector reluctantly revealed that on the night of the first collapse, Lord Hanuman or Anjaneya, the monkey god, believed to be the ancient guardian deity of the Kaveri Delta's rice fields, had appeared to him in a dream. The deity told him, 'My idol is lying under the broken span in the riverbed. Unearth it and make me a shrine there that I may guard this bridge across the waters as I am meant to for the welfare of the people.'

'I would not have mentioned it if the span had not collapsed for the third time, even after all the care we've taken,' said the construction inspector, greatly embarrassed but too worried to hold back, for the serial collapses defied all logic.

Not unnaturally, Capt. J.L. Calddell, the British engineer in charge, laughed at this fanciful story. But he himself had a terrible dream that night about menacing monkeys. It was so vivid that he told his fellow officers about it the next day and was scoffed at in turn. The engineer was glad to be persuaded that it was all nonsense but despaired of a practical solution. That night he dreamed again of monkeys but Lord Hanuman appeared as well, and told him kindly, 'Make a bend in your structure at the spot and make a small shrine to me there. That will hold up the span.'

This was so uncannily precise that the next day, without further ado, the engineer had his team excavate under the rubble and there, under the nineteenth span, lay the promised idol, more of a square slab of granite really, with a lively figure of Lord Hanuman carved on it in the temple style of over a thousand years ago. Was it a relic of those times that had been disturbed? Who knew but that this idol's time had come to see the light of day? After three spectacular and mysterious collapses, the engineer was taking no chances. A shrine was built at once, its consecration speedily performed and the British addition to the Anicut was remodelled as directed in Captain Calddell's dream.

It has been 200 years since these curious events took place along the 2000-year-old canal and the bridge is holding up well. Those days the British government paid for the monthly puja or worship at Hanuman's temple and the Indian government pays for it now. You can find this story in the *Tanjore District Gazetteer* of those years and in the Silver Jubilee souvenir (2008) of the Kaveri Delta Farmers' Welfare Association, where it is retold with honour as the legitimate lore of the land. Perhaps it was this incident that inspired Rudyard Kipling's nineteenth-century story, 'The Bridge-Builders'.

Every year, before the planting of the bhogam or first paddy crop, the farmers ceremonially offer the paddy seeds to Hanuman at this shrine and then to the waters. Only then is the water for irrigation released from the sluices.

16

The songs in his heart

Back in the year 1525, deep in the south of India, a family of musicians looked forward to the birth of a child, as families usually do. They were instrumental musicians who served at temples and their community was known as the Isai Vellalar, or literally 'those who grow music'. This family lived in the Tamil town of Sirkali in the Kaveri Delta and revered Lord Shiva as Koothan, the cosmic dancer, at his ninth-century temple in Chidambaram. This ancient temple town was across the River Kollidam from Sirkali and the only place in India that depicted Shiva as the dancer.

If they had a boy, the family planned to name him after Lord Shiva as 'Thandavan', or the 'one who dances the Thandavam'—the cosmic dance that is believed to keep the universe going. It was a philosophical concept about energy, which was expressed symbolically through beautiful bronze statues of the dancing god. Each detail of such statues had its own iconic meaning and layers of mythology to it that were well known through oral tradition, so much so that a statue was like a book to both the educated and to those who could not read.

But the child, when he arrived, was a terrible disappointment to his family. He was weak, sickly and unappealing. He was unable to eat properly and did not grow strong. Theirs was a handsome family, proud of its musical talent and its place of honour at the temple and in society. They were ashamed and angry that their son, their heir, who should have made everyone envy them, was a liability and not an asset. He was clearly unfit to become a temple musician and a person of note. So Thandavan's position in his family, which should have been sky-high because he was the son, fell to the bottom because he was sickly.

All this open disapproval took its toll on the boy's nerves. He developed a severe skin infection all over his body. Pustules oozed from him and not even powders from the brilliant local Siddha healer or baths in medicinal water boiled with vepe or margosa leaves could rid him of the hideous rash. His family began to absolutely loathe him and the little boy became even more sickly and silent.

His only friend was a musical neighbour called Shivabhagyam, the lady of the house next door. Shivabhagyam, which means, 'auspicious luck', always had a kind word to say to Thandavan. She invited him home to watch when she did her daily puja to Shiva and sang many songs to him about the great god.

Shivabhagyam's family was even better off than Thandavan's, and Thandavan's family hated that she was good to him. They took it as a personal affront. How could they stop her? They came up with the diabolical idea of throwing him out of the house. If he no longer lived with them, he could not visit next door. Nor would the kaval or town watchmen let anyone loiter on a residential street.

Driven out of home by his own parents with abuses and curses, the boy's already precarious world wholly tumbled down about his ears. He gathered such shreds of dignity as were left to him and silently made his way to the local Shiva temple at Sirkali. He sat down at the very end of the ranks of beggars outside the temple. Unwilling to hold his hand out to anyone, he subsisted on scraps of the temple's prasad that fell to him or the bananas or pieces of coconut and jaggery dropped before him by some passing pilgrim, and grew sicker by the day.

One hot afternoon, he crawled for shade into the temple's storeroom where the palanquins were kept. They were used to taking around images of Shiva and Parvati, the temple's presiding deities, in procession on big festival days. The tall, carved, granite pillars and walls of the temple storeroom made for a cool cave. Weak with hunger, the boy fainted in a corner. After the evening worship, the priests put out the oil lamps and torches and locked up for the night, not knowing about the unconscious refugee in there. Coming to in the dark after an hour or so, Thandavan called out in a faint voice to the gods and lay back exhausted.

By and by a little girl appeared, carrying a tray which bore an earthen lamp, a bowl of rice and vegetables and a small water pot. She called out in a bright, affectionate way to Thandavan and peering timidly out from behind a palanquin, he saw that it was the priest's little daughter. She fed and comforted the boy and as she turned to leave, advised him to go every day to Chidambaram and compose a new song to Shiva with the first words he heard spoken in the temple there. Greatly cheered, Thandavan went to sleep.

The next day, when the storeroom was unlocked, Thandavan stepped out, apologizing humbly to the priests for having fallen asleep in there. But the priests looked at him open-mouthed in awe. Gone were the wounds, gone was his loathsome skin and his sickly appearance. Not only was he healed but his skin glowed with such lustre that they wonderingly named him 'Muthu Thandavar', which meant 'pearl' with the honorific 'r' at the end of his name. But when the boy told them about the priest's daughter, it was a mystery that no one could solve. She had stayed snug at home the previous evening and nobody knew who the little girl with the tray was.

The boy looked gratefully at his soft, clear skin and thought it must have been Parvati, worshipped in Sirkali as 'Lokanayaki', or the heroine of the world, who had come to him disguised. The priests invited him to make his home in the temple's rest house. Thandavan thanked them gladly and said he would come back every day but that he had undertaken a vow to visit Chidambaram each morning. He did not share the reason just then, afraid that he was incapable of composing even one song. With a profound salute to the deities of Sirkali, Thandavan crossed the River Kollidam to Chidambaram.

His first song began with the words, '*Bhuloka Kailayagiri Chidambaram*', meaning 'Chidambaram is Mount Kailash on earth'—the first words that he heard at the temple, an exclamation by an ecstatic devotee as he walked in. Five gold pieces of great antiquity appeared at the deity's feet after the song was sung, creating an uproar. Had a rich merchant made an offering, unnoticed, wondered the priests. But why had he chosen to stay silent when they asked whose offering it was? Was it perhaps from a devout thief who had quietly given Shiva a portion of his loot as penance?

Thandavan felt that it was yet another miracle; precious gold coins appearing mysteriously like that at the deity's feet the moment he had finished his song. He felt elated to think that god had rewarded him for keeping his dignity even through the most dire straits. Koothan Shiva had let everyone know that now Thandavan was as good as anybody else and worth appreciating.

Many songs followed after that and Thandavar strove sincerely to keep his daily tryst with Shiva. Once, when the Kollidam was in furious spate and he was unable to cross, he sang the still-famous song, 'The day has been wasted that I can't see You' in the rich old musical scale, Dhanyasi.

The story goes that the floodwaters receded and let him cross.

One morning, to his great confusion, not a word was spoken in the temple. All Thandavar could hear was his own heartbeat pounding in his ears. He cried aloud, 'Be still, my heart' and so composed the day's song with his own words.

His creative dependence on others was over.

Serene in his own strength now, Thandavar left his childhood behind forever. He often wondered, though, about the transformative night in the Sirkali temple storeroom. He had almost died that night, at the very end of his tether. Perhaps he had ached so intensely to be healed and to prove himself that the deepest wish of his heart had manifested to him and shown him the way. He was glad it was through a vision of the beautiful gods. It struck him that he had given up wholly on earthly ties that night; and in the sheltering darkness of the temple, he had cast himself upon fate.

Free in his mind, happy in his music and poetry, grateful for his food and shelter and deeply pleased that his songs were appreciated,

Thandavar had no anger or grief left for those who had been so shatteringly unkind to him. They had become as unreal to him as if they were people met by someone else, not him, in another life. Knowing their true worth, he never deceived himself with expectations and kept his emotional and physical distance from them, though he did not hold back from meeting his first kind helper, Shivabhagyam. The townsfolk were drawn to him, however, sure of a kindly word. Knowing that he had suffered greatly himself, they were not afraid to let down their guard with him and let him see their own vulnerability and he passed the rest of his life in great peace The legend goes that one day, in 1600, a great light shone in Shiva's sanctum at Chidambaram and Mutthu Thandavar, an old man by then, disappeared into it. Aptly, it was the anniversary of the day that Shiva is said to have first danced the Thandavam at Chidambaram.

17

The promissory note

The national anthem of India, *Jana Gana Mana*, has unsuspected layers of story and myth attached almost incidentally to it. For instance, it is set to a tune that is but a note away from the hoary musical scale, Raga Shankarabharanam, which is its name in south India. In the north, this scale goes by the name Raag Bilawal. Great twentieth-century musicians of the northern tradition have sung this noble scale with relish, especially Kumar Gandharva and Pandit Mallikarjun Mansur of Dharwar. Ustad Nissar Ahmed Khan of the Rampur-Seheswan gharana or style of music is said to have moved the public to tears when he sang *'Sumiran kar man Ram naam'* in Bilawal ('O my heart, remember Lord Ram's name with devoted love').

In the 1820s, at the royal court of Thanjavur, Shankarabharanam produced such ecstasy that Raja Sarfoji, the Maratha king, declared that the singer, Narasaiyer, would be called 'Shankarabharanam Narasaiyer' from that day, and so he became known throughout south India.

Once, when Narasaiyer badly needed a loan, he went to Rambhadra Moopanar, the zamindar of a place called Kapisthalam. Moopanar had proved a generous and hospitable patron to many musicians in the Kaveri Delta and Narasaiyer felt he could approach him. But, puffed up with pride, Narasaiyer spoke pompously to the zamindar. For eighty English gold guineas, he grandly offered Raga Shankarabharanam as collateral with a promissory note not to sing it until he had redeemed his debt. Hurt by Narasaiyer's attitude, the zamindar was equally businesslike and accepted the promissory note the singer gave him.

Soon after this unholy bargain, a powerful employee of the East India Company called 'Wallis' Appuraya, after his English boss, invited Narasaiyer to a concert in the neighbouring town of Kumbakonam. There was a wedding in Appuraya's family and many singers of note were invited to perform for the guests. This was the custom at weddings in well-off homes across south India, to have a concert of classical music both as a treat and as a benediction, for music was considered the gift of the gods. The singer arrived with his accompanists at Appuraya's large mansion, where he was very hospitably accommodated. After lunch, the host discussed the concert with Narasaiyer and said how much he looked forward to hearing Shankarabharanam sung that evening. In fact, he wanted the concert to open with it.

'But I can't,' said the singer, greatly embarrassed. 'I've pledged not to sing it until I can redeem my debt to the zamindar of Kapisthalam.'

'Bah, is that all?' said Appuraya and sent eighty gold guineas by a swift rider to the landlord.

The messenger came back to Appuraya with Moopanar hot on his heels. He had rushed over from Kapisthalam not only to return Appuraya's money but also to chide the singer for not demanding the money as a right. These generous and diplomatic gestures by the two big men saved face all around and brought home to Narasaiyer how very silly and vain he had been to think that he owned the great raga. It was merely his good luck that he had presented it creditably enough to be awarded an association with it by King Sarfoji. A charming royal whim, no more but Narasaiyer had gone and fallen for his own publicity.

The raga was an intangible spiritual and aesthetic being, he realized. It belonged only to itself and to the people at large. To try and 'own' it was uncultured and impertinent. He could only hope to explore the music as well as his imagination and skill let him.

Deciding to deal with his shame and chagrin after his professional demands were met, Narasaiyer sang his heart out at Appuraya's concert. Applauded wildly and presented with rich shawls, bags of gold, jewelled bracelets and rings, he responded with modesty and composure while his heart smote him that he had demeaned himself and betrayed his music. He left quietly the next morning, pretending to go home but went instead to the temple town of Kivalur that lay towards Nagapattinam.

An incredible story had rocked south India about Kivalur. The tale went that the Carnatic saint-composer, Muthuswami Dikshithar had gone to the exquisite Shiva temple in Kivalur with a song in Shankarabharanam bursting out of his head. He arrived just as the priest on duty had wound up after morning worship and was preparing to shut the enormous carved wooden doors. Dikshithar politely asked the priest if he could wait a few minutes to let him present at least the bare bones of his song to the god. But the priest curtly refused. He locked up and stalked away saying, 'You can just as well wait until we reopen in the afternoon. The deity isn't going anywhere, you know.'

So Dikshithar sat down calmly, and facing the closed doors, bowed to the god from outside and began to sing '*Akshaya linga vibho*', his majestic new composition praising Shiva in Shankarabharanam. Passers-by were drawn at once to the music and sat down to listen as if under a spell. Dikshithar unhurriedly sang it all, with every variation adding another rich layer to the song. Gods, angels, soldiers, singers, dancers and drummers seemed to form a glorious company in that song and every flowering plant, every soft breeze and every laughing stream found place in it too. The magical soundscape drew everyone into itself and they felt their hurt and sorrows fading and their hearts began to feel healed and whole. They felt bold and empowered and absurdly happy in the sanctuary of sound.

There was deep silence when the song ended. But before the crowd could come out of its enchantment to clap or cry '*Shabash!*', the locked temple doors crashed open and swung heavily on their medieval iron hinges. A collective gasp went up and the priest, who had hung back to see what was going on, rushed forward in tears. He fell at Dikshithar's feet and said how very sorry he was.

The story had spread from coast to coast and Narasaiyer thought Kivalur was the right place in which to make his own apologies to Raga Shankarabharanam.

Arriving at the Kivalur temple, Narasaiyer prayed to Shiva to forgive him for his vanity and to the spirit of the raga for his presumption. He found himself a quiet corner of the temple courtyard and meditated on the god and the raga. He recalled that 'Shankar-Abharanam' meant 'Shiva's ornament' in Sanskrit. An old text called the *Brahmanda Purana* told of how Narada, the wandering sage, had once stopped by a place called Bhadragiri and worshipped Shiva there by playing Shankarabharanam on his divine lute. Narada had greatly pleased Shiva by playing Shankarabharanam for the raga was close to the lord's heart. Besides being beautiful, it was a healing raga, and Shiva was also worshipped as Vaidisvaran, Lord of Healers. Many people spoke of how well and strong they felt after being immersed in listening to Shankarabharanam.

Thinking over the myths and legends that vivified the land and the close, powerful ties that its people had with their music, Narasaiyer began to feel healed himself. The world was the most enormous stage and everybody had their turn and went away, whereas the music stayed on forever. Freed of anxiety by this perspective, he went home. He quietly renounced the title of 'Shankarabharanam Narasaiyer' and became an even better singer for it.

18

The old man and the sea

Everyone knows about the earthquake and tsunami in the Indian Ocean that wrecked parts of India's southeast coast and parts of South East Asia in December 2006. But a tsunami that hit coastal Tamil Nadu, most probably in the second century CE, is not well known and does not figure in the list of historical tsunamis of ancient times. This may be because the text in which it is mentioned was discovered only in the late nineteenth century. The text is the Tamil epic, *Manimekhalai*, which scholars date back to the second century CE.

That ancient tsunami swallowed up the fabled port of Poompuhar or Puhar, the Blossom City, not far from present-day Nagapattinam.

Because it happened so long ago, we cannot begin to imagine what that ancestral tsunami must have been like. By ancient accounts, Puhar was an international port of call for ships from many countries in the old universe of discourse.

The tsunami belt stretched all the way from Puhar to Japan where Buddhist monks had sailed from India taking their stories with them. This story from Japan that sounds so much like a Jataka in its mood and message stands in for Puhar's tsunami stories that are presumed to be lost to time.

It seems there was once an antisocial old man who lived alone atop a hill. He had been married once and had had children but they had all died young. After some years the man retreated to the top of the hill above his village, which was by the sea. He had fallen very comfortably into the habit of solitude and went down to the village only when he absolutely had to go, to trade and shop.

The villagers were used to him and accepted his taciturn ways with a shrug. Three generations had grown up in the years he had lived on the hill and when someone asked how long he had been up there, the villagers answered, 'Always.'

The old man felt he had good reason to despise his fellow beings. Their stupid, vain chatter about unimportant things, their petty quarrels and jealousies, their mean thefts and malicious tongues made them ugly in his eyes.

The old man preferred his own company by far. He caught fish in the little mountain stream below his hut, harvested his few, carefully tended peach trees, grew enough rice for himself on a few terraces in his backyard and made sure to grow plenty of vegetables. He wove his own cloth and dried his home-made noodles on a wooden frame that he had made himself. He ate his simple meals from a wooden bowl with chopsticks that he had carved. Afterwards, he would stare contentedly out to sea while sipping tea, and remembered to thank the Daibutsu or Lord Buddha for his good health and good life. He listened to birdsong and watched the clouds shift shape and colour. Like all those who spend a lot of time outdoors and absorb many impressions of light and shade, he could instinctively tell you to the half-hour what time of day it was.

One morning, his eye was caught by a new rock far out from the shore. The water seemed to have rolled right back to this rock. The old man frowned, trying to recall a tale that his grandfather had told him of his own youth long ago. Just so, the water had receded far back until a submerged rock suddenly revealed itself. Soon after, the sea sprung out in a gigantic wave to swallow the village and miles of the countryside.

The old man suddenly remembered that the annual fair for which the whole village gathered on the beach was that very day. He forgot about being antisocial. A greater power called human duty seized him. Too far away to do anything else, he ran to collect every wooden thing he had and as much straw as he could find, piled it all inside and set his hut on fire. Seeing the smoke and the blaze, the villagers cried out in alarm and ran uphill in a body to save his life. Seconds after they reached the safety of the hilltop, the tsunami engulfed the beach and everything below.

19

The golden goose

'Once upon a time', goes the ancient Jataka of the Suvanna Hansa or 'the golden goose', when Brahmadatta was the Kashi Naresh or King of Benares, the Bodhisattva was born as a priest. He married according to custom and produced three daughters, whom he named Nanda, Nandavati and Sundarinanda. Unusually, for an Indian father, he did not pine for sons but loved his family of girls dearly. Although he was a poor priest who had been raised on the town's charity as expended at the pathshala or Vedic school, he took his responsibility as a householder seriously and did his duty as prescribed, by feeding travellers and the poor as best as he was able to. He was also keenly aware of his duty as a father and while his wife trained their daughters in the domestic arts and in dressing neatly, and as nicely as their circumstances allowed, the Bodhisattva set himself to provide for their weddings. He worked very hard, making himself available as a priest for every ritual that marked every rite of passage observed by the citizenry. He never stopped working and by and by, he wore himself out.

When he took ill and died, his wife and daughters were cast helpless on the world. They could no longer pay the rent for their modest home in the priests' quarters and were accommodated for their father's sake in a corner of the dharamshala or public rest house attached to the temple. They had been content with their lot as a poor but complete family, happy in their simple life. But without a father or brother to go out and earn, they found that even their small security was gone forever. Nobody would employ them as servants for they were too pretty and besides, they were modest and timid. Heroines they emphatically were not, just regular girls who had suddenly fallen below the poverty line and were now homeless and destitute. The townsfolk were too embarrassed to employ the priest's widow and daughters to clean and cook, and instead, gave them leftover food. If anyone remembered, the little family got a set of simple new clothes for Dipavali once a year. It was a double bind. Though the girls were willing to work as servants, nobody was willing to employ them; though pretty, and capable as homemakers, nobody wanted to marry them because they were too poor to host even the most modest wedding feast. Indeed, they barely managed to subsist by living on charity.

Meanwhile, the Bodhisattva was reborn as a golden goose that remembered its past life. It went back to its former family in Kashi and when it found them alone, it spoke in a human voice. It told them to pluck out one golden feather from its body every few days to sell and live by. The mother and daughters wept over the beautiful bird and shrinkingly pulled out a feather, apologizing for causing the hansa pain. They went to the local goldsmith and told him that the golden feather had floated down to them from heaven. With the money they got for the golden feather, they bought food and clothes and rented a small room to live in.

This went on very well for some months but one day, their landlord asked them to move elsewhere for he needed their room for his own relatives. Instead of taking this coolly and calmly as a minor upheaval, the Bodhisattva's former wife had a terrible anxiety attack recalling their bad times. She conspired with her daughters to pluck the golden goose bare of all its feathers in case it flew away and never came back. The hansa shed tears at their foolishness and lack of appreciation for its commitment to them. But it was helpless to stop their vandalism and it gave up its life, having fulfilled its duty to them even in its next birth. There was only this much a person could do to protect his family. Having delivered its terse message that everyone should think things through before acting hastily, the Jataka does not tell us what became of Nanda, Nandavati,

Sundarinanda and their mother. But their fate has haunted us down the ages. Did they have to move to another town to find work? Perhaps they managed to get a life after all, having learnt this terrible lesson.

20

The performance

When Narasa Nayaka or 'Narasimha Nayak' was high king of Vijayanagar, he encouraged poets and performers to wander about his empire in south India and refresh his hard-working subjects with wit and verse, song and dance, and especially with stories of the resplendent gods. Scholars and artistes were welcomed at his court and the royal chamberlain of the great palace at Hampi, the capital, was in charge of the cultural events selected for a 'command performance'.

One time, soon after the rigours and restrictions of the chaturmaas or monsoon season were over, when it was feasible for the common folk to travel again by foot, palanquin, horse and bullock cart, a programme at court was announced as usual. It was to be a brahmana mela or play performed by the priests of the village of Kuchelapuram, from the banks of the River Krishna. They were to present the *Prahlada Charitram*, in which a horrid mythical tyrant was routed by Lord Vishnu in his avatar as Narasimha, the man–lion. Such dance–dramas or operas, which were a blend of speech and songs, were a very old tradition of India.

Each region had developed exciting art forms of its own, marrying local arts with epic stories.

Before the time of Vijayanagar, in the days of the preceding Kakatiya dynasty, the artistes of the southern lands had excelled in *Shiva Leela*, or episodes that illumined the tales of the great god Shiva. Over time, the complex lore of his divine confrère Lord Vishnu, had become very popular too for the stories were exceedingly enactable with interesting plots and subplots. The troupe from Kuchelapuram was made up of artistes who could speak in Telugu and Sanskrit and could sing

Carnatic music, with gifted young men playing female characters.

Narasa Nayaka and his court looked forward to that evening's entertainment in the sandalwood-scented, rosewater-sprinkled courtyard. The courtyard had long strings of jasmine looped around its granite pillars while finely chased brass holders of sambrani smoked in the corners, the fragrant resin burnt on live coals to keep away mosquitoes and insects.

Into this expectant, fire-lit atmosphere, with a roll of drums stepped the artistes of Kuchelapuram, bowing in deep namaste to Narasa Nayaka and his court. The prologue began, invoking the guardians of the eight directions and the grace of the powers of justice and righteousness. 'A delicate compliment to our capable king and his good governance,' thought his ministers, preening a little, for were they not part of it?

'Unusual,' thought the king, for plays normally had an invocation to Shiva, Vishnu or Ganesha.

The hero, Prahlada, played by a pale, resolute-looking youth, remonstrated with his tyrannical father, the titan Hiranya Kashyap. 'I cannot submit to you as my guru, O Raja,' he said firmly. 'You are the king of my region, no doubt. But the king of my heart is that just, righteous and merciful One, the Lord who abides in his victorious city.'

'Why, that's "Vijayanagar", the "victorious city",' thought Narasa Nayaka, suddenly intent.

'He is too far away in his kingdom to save you, Prahlada,' boomed the titan. 'I am the one with absolute and immediate power over you.'

'He is a gentle lord,' said Prahlada, turning to face Narasa Nayaka and bowing deeply. 'Unlike you, he is not feared by his subjects. He does not tax them cruelly, or make them yield their fields and gold to you, or forcibly take their sons away to serve as soldiers or demand their wives and daughters for his own inner chambers.'

'How I choose to rule is not your business, son,' thundered the tyrant king. 'Your only task is to address me in your prayers, for I alone am God Almighty, not this faraway Vishnu on his faraway throne.'

'Very specific points under that epic tone,' thought Narasa Nayaka, his interest fairly caught.

The play went on, its intensity growing with every scene as Hiranya Kashyap, fed up with his unyielding son, tried every trick in the epic book to kill him and failed, for each time, 'faraway Vishnu on his faraway throne' saved his devotee.

The play climaxed with Vishnu erupting from a pillar as Narasimha, the fierce man-lion, to disembowel the tyrant king, and triumphant songs and a shower of rose petals marked its close.

The king graciously bestowed the customary bags of gold, silk shawls and gold bracelets on the old priest with the enigmatic face who was the troupe leader and retired to his palace to think it over.

The next morning, he summoned his prime minister and army chief.

'We have some very interesting subjects in our empire,' he told them with a grim smile. 'The artistes of Kuchelapuram will need an armed escort to go home; make it a fairly big escort and well-armed. They have risked their lives to convey their message to me indirectly through their art and thankfully, I could read between the lines. Prime Minister, please send an able administrator with the armed escort. Acting on your authority, he will depose and imprison Guruva Raju, the chieftain, who presently administers the region, and take his place. The armed escort must stay with the new administrator. Guruva Raju's coffers must be inspected and all wealth that rightfully belongs to the royal treasury must be seized and dispatched to Hampi, as must any stockpile of arms and ammunition. The citizens held in service by constraint must be set free, their names must be recorded and an honorarium disbursed to them to go home with. After these matters are taken care of, a healing puja must be conducted, addressed to Lord Vishnu to thank him for his grace and favour on our land. All citizens of the region must be invited to the feast at the temple and there must be a parade by representatives of all the guilds and communities with singers and dancers leading them, to celebrate their release from bondage in a befitting manner.'

The performance

And so it was. The *Machupalli Kaifiat*, a record of the region from 1502, tells us the gist of this story about the resource and daring of the artistes of Kuchelapuram, later known as Kuchipudi.

21

A kingdom won

This tale concerns one of the very oldest royal houses in the world, whose story has gone under the debris of time. Trigarta was an ancient kingdom that finds honourable mention in the Ramayana and the Mahabharata, and in a later text, the *Brahmanda Purana*. In the Mahabharata, the kings of Trigarta are described as sworn territorial enemies of Matsya, a kingdom allied to the Pandavas. So they fought them under their first cousin, Duryodhana, on the Kaurava side in the Battle of Kurukshetra. Susharma, the Trigarta raja, led a do-or-die squadron called the Samsaptaka to capture the senior-most Pandava prince, Yudhishtir. He, and his entire akshauhini or battalion, were finished off by the Pandava prince, Arjuna.

Just so, in the Ramayana, had the Trigarta rajas fought and lost to Sri Ram, the prince of Ayodhya.

The Trigartas are described as nobles of the Chandravanshi or Lunar Dynasty. The Katoch Rajputs who claim descent from the Trigartas, founded the kingdom of Kangra in the hills to the east of the Punjab plains. The first-known Katoch raja was Bhumi Chand, and in the *Brahmanda Purana*, he is said to have built the original temple to the goddess Parvati at Jawalamukhi in the Kangra Valley. It was then known as 'Jalandhara'.

A scion of this ancient clan called Hari Chand founded the scenic hill kingdom of Guler sometime in the fifteenth century. Like most princes and feudal chiefs around the world, Hari Chand loved the hunt. Bear, deer and leopards were the sport of hill rajas though they had rules about when and what to hunt. It was thought unsportsman-like to hunt newborn cubs and fawns but full-grown animals were fair game. Behold Raja Hari Chand then, one fine day in late summer, out hunting deer in the thickly forested hillsides beyond Guler Fort. His quarry led him on a long chase and the king left his companions far behind. Deeper and deeper into the forest went the king and the deer lured him on, seeming more and more like the fabled golden deer in the Ramayana. Along the way, the king found the remains of an old human settlement deep in a grove. Were these rotted timbers the supports of an old forest ashram from long ago? Crossing the site, the king's foot slipped and before he knew it, he found he had fallen about 20 feet into a smooth, deep hole. 'A dry well,' thought Raja Hari Chand, before his head struck a rock and he passed out. The grass that hid the well closed over it again. The grove returned to its primordial soundscape of insects and the sudden soft stir made by some passing animal.

Meanwhile, the king's companions searched the forest, growing increasingly afraid. One of them rushed back to the fort to get reinforcements. The king's younger brother, the prime minister, the head of the army and a select band of soldiers and trackers went looking for him. After days of desperate search, they were forced to mourn the king as dead. His younger brother was crowned the new raja of Guler.

Months into the new reign, the court was disturbed one day by a great commotion in the forecourt. Into a shocked silence walked Raja Hari Chand, leaner, scarred and dressed in the simplest of clothes. But it was the king all right. The courtiers sprang up as one man with a great shout and the new king ran forward to hug his elder brother and touch his feet. Tears in his eyes, he bowed low as behoved him and indicated the throne so that the rightful king, magically restored, could take his place.

But the Katoch had been kings for millennia and were not arrivistes at the game of thrones. The king of Guler, Raja Hari Chand, refused to take back the kingdom that was rightfully his. Life had ordained that his younger brother should sit on the throne and to take it away now seemed both wrong and impractical. The entire court had realigned itself as any system will with a new head. It was miracle enough that wandering gypsies had found him, recognized him from seeing him ride out in royal processions, stayed in the forest to nurse him through concussion, delirium, fever and the long convalescence in which he was too weak to walk, and brought him home.

'Have we not heard enough and seen enough of brother fighting brother for the throne?' said Raja Hari Chand to his amazed younger brother and his court. 'With your permission, I will make myself another fort below Guler, down on the river flats by the Banganga.' In this diplomatic way, with one graceful move and with maximum damage control, he not only regained his own status but retained his brother as an ally, not an enemy. The royal priest and the prime minster forbore to meet each other's eyes and looked at Hari Chand with respect. This was a royal retrieve indeed and a bad situation had been neatly side-stepped.

139

22

The scent of her hair

Nakkeeran was born to a family of conch-cutters
that specialized in a craft dedicated to the Supreme
Goddess who presided over Madurai. Her throat
was famously praised to be 'as smooth as a conch'
and the people of Madurai, a set of persons
addicted to sweet sounds, smells and sights, set
great store by smooth, silky skin in one another.
Though a sturdy race, with spears blunted in
many a territorial battle and markets known as
notable centres of trade, the people of Madurai
were spoilt and sensitive, leading a very good life
in their rich, green land nourished by the River
Vaigai. They cherished their singers, dancers and

141

poets and celebrated every vizha or festival with a flourish of grand processions.

Drummers and dancers took the lead in their processions and there were marchers bearing flowered arches and silken banners on long poles, tumblers and conjurors and winsome troupes of transgender acrobats and beautiful public women that the whole region came to see as living works of art. The country folk drove into town on bright, jingling carts drawn by sharp-horned cattle, the carpenters, leather-workers, potters, stone-masons and weavers walked proudly in guilds, as did the traders, merchants and soldiers who threw out their chests on parade, and everywhere along the way the people cheered and cheered and threw jasmine buds and golden champaka flowers at them, celebrating the blissful life of Madurai before they went home to great feasts of spiced mutton, rice, vegetables and fruit.

Madurai was especially famous as the epicentre of poetry, and the traditions of the old Sangam or Academy Era of fine verse were by no means entirely over when Nakkeeran found a place at King Nedumaran's court as a poet of eminence, becoming over time the leader of the academy. Anybody who could compose well enough had a claim on the court and on the academy that set the standard for language and literature.

Being deeply in love with his queen, King Nedumaran decided one day to hold a poetry competition on the eternally pleasing theme of 'woman', with a bag of gold coins for the winner as the prize. The town crier made the announcement and Madurai began to hum as contenders set to work, scribbling on palm leaves or striding up and down on the banks of the Vaigai hoping for inspiration. Nobody could talk of anything else; the prestige and the prize attached to it awoke the competitive spirit in every poet and would-be-poet. In this hubbub, on the day before the poets' assembly, a poor and not particularly bright poet called Dharmi, or 'Tharumi' in the graceful Madurai accent, wandered into the great temple in which Shiva was worshipped as Kaal Adinathar, the Lord of Time.

The temple was closed for the afternoon but Tharumi wanted a private word with god and slipped in quietly. He sat down facing the main inner shrine, his back to a carved granite thoon or pillar.

'You're a fine one,' he told the god, who lurked at ease behind the doors of his shrine, sure of being offered camphor, water, milk, bilva leaves and quantities of fruit and flowers several times a day. 'You're the Father of the World, but you don't seem to care that I'm so poor and hopelessly inadequate as a poet. Nor have I the skill to apply myself to another trade. This city expects everyone to be very good at what they do, particularly poetry, and looks down on untalented people like me. And it's your fault for setting such high standards for Madurai. Did you have to hold the first ever Sangam of antiquity here in my city?'

The discouraging silence that followed this rant did not deter Tharumi; he went on reproaching Shiva. 'Isn't it time you took a hand in improving my fortune?' he asked piteously at the end and stared hard at the shrine with equal love and despair.

A little cough sounded behind him and Tharumi saw an old man standing between the pillars, holding out a palm leaf.

'A verse for you, then,' said the mysterious old man cordially with the faintest wink, handing it over to the gawping complainant. 'I'm sure you'll win the king's prize.' And as is the norm in these matters, he vanished suddenly.

Tharumi went home, his heart pounding with excitement, and managed to find a clean set of clothes that he ironed with the heated base of a round, brass water pot.

Poets' assembly day! Almost all of Madurai was gathered in the big forecourt of the great temple near the temple tank. The king sat on a decorated stone platform ringed by the leading members of the academy, while a spot was marked onstage for each competitor to come and declaim his verse by turn. All too soon, it was Tharumi's chance, which came at the end. He blinked when roars of applause greeted his verse, the king applauding loudest of all.

'Such felicity of word and thought, the prize must go to you,' said the king graciously, while the academy members nodded benignly. But Nakkeeran stood up and said, 'No, Your Majesty.'

'Why not, noble poet?' said the king, still gracious.

'There is a fault in his verse. He speaks of "the natural fragrance of a woman's hair", which, as you know, simply does not exist. The fragrance comes from the flowers she wears in her hair, from perfumed hair oil, from scented soap nut powder or from the incense-like smoke of the sambrani resin that is burnt on live coals to dry her hair with. While the academy grants a due measure of poetic licence in such earthbound themes, it is not our custom to mislead the public with incorrect information. For instance, in a poem about the kurinji or mountain region, we speak of the flower that blooms naturally there, of the dazzling kurinji flower that blooms once in twelve years. To serve a rhyme, we do not forcibly transplant the water lily of the neydhal or coast, to the mountains, or the other way around. So I submit that this man's poem does not qualify for the prize—or even as a poem.'

Tharumi looked wildly at the faces around him that had beamed approval a moment ago and were now curling with scorn.

'This is not my poem!' he stuttered. 'Please wait, I'll fetch the man who gave it to me,' and bolted before anyone could stop him. The king shrugged and other poems shortlisted by the academy began to be reviewed.

Meanwhile, Tharumi ran into the temple and began to pound on the pillars with his fists, wailing to Shiva to rescue him from certain death. The old man obligingly appeared on cue and led the way back to the assembly, telling Tharumi to calm down.

Striding up to the platform, the old man, with Tharumi stumbling behind, made his way boldly to the king, bowed low to him and coolly asked Nakkeeran what the problem was.

Nakkeeran, at a nod from King Nedumaran, repeated his objection.

'Very well,' said the old man smoothly. 'Perhaps not in the case of an ordinary woman. But surely the queen of our fair realm may be said to have a natural fragrance to her hair?'

The crowd gasped at the impertinence, while the king frowned and regretted that he had chosen such a double-edged sword of a theme, and some of Nakkeeran's jealous ill-wishers in the academy thought with grim satisfaction, 'Now let the old curmudgeon get out of that.'

But, 'No,' said Nakkeeran, with frigid politeness. 'I'm afraid not. Our noble queen, though the queen, is nevertheless a mortal woman.'

'What about the celestial maidens then, the apsaras?' said the old man, smiling faintly in appreciation of this irrefutable snub.

'We have no means of verifying that possibility,' said Nakkeeran, annoyingly to the point again. The king laughed suddenly and so did a few members of the academy, while the crowd chuckled openly at this comprehensive put-down.

Tharumi stole a look at the old man and suddenly cried out in fear. The old man stood very straight now and his limbs shone with unearthly lustre. He looked to be furious and a vertical crease had appeared in the middle of his forehead that glowed a fiery red.

'The Lord God,' whimpered Tharumi and fell to his knees. The king, his courtiers and the citizens exclaimed in shock and awe and sank to their knees too. Only Nakkeeran was left standing and bowed composedly to the old man, who bore the unmistakable signs of being Lord Shiva himself.

'Tell me, Nakkeeran,' said the old man sternly into the silence, with a look at cowed, kneeling Madurai. 'You worship Parvati, don't you, as Poon Kodai, the Goddess with flowers in her hair, in this very city, and Shiva, as the Lord of Time? They are your personal deities. You dedicate your words and deeds to them every single day. Would you go so far as to say that even Parvati has no natural fragrance to her hair?'

Nakkeeran stood still, thinking. Shiva was clearly playing one of his mystifying games and he, Nakkeeran, must find his lines and play along, risking all.

He looked his god in the eye and said politely but firmly, 'Even if it's the Lord with the eye in his forehead, a fault is a fault.'

149

Nakkeeran had very properly refused to be drawn into an unseemly debate about the goddess, in whose praise no words and no flights of worshipful fancy were good enough, and thrown the ball right back at Shiva. The crowd sighed hearing him and closed its eyes, unable to look.

It's said that Nakkeeran then took a flying leap into the temple tank to escape the blaze from Shiva's third eye; that annihilating look that had incinerated Kama, the God of Love, that fiery blaze from which Kumar, the War Lord, was born. But he came to no harm for Shiva liked it that Nakkeeran, though a puny mortal, had stood up to him with such polite conviction and even indirectly rebuked him for having bandied Goddess Parvati's name about in an unbecoming manner. As a matter of fact, Shiva went away greatly pleased that a lesson had been imparted to all to think things through, respond appropriately, and not take even a god's word for it.

The king gave the bag of gold to Nakkeeran for his immense courage and for having enabled them all to obtain a glimpse of the great god; and in thanksgiving to Shiva for having spared him, Nakkeeran entreated the king to spare Tharumi and gave half the gold to the lying poet, although it was not his poem at all and remained as faulty as ever.

23

Manohra, the bird princess

The next time you're on the approach road to Suvarnabhumi Airport in Bangkok, you might want to look again at the statues of golden bird people with their hands folded in wai (namaste). They are images of kinnara and kinnari, the half-human, half-avian creatures of shared Indic myth who excel in song and dance and live in the celestial forest of Himavan.

This story about a kinnari is a Thai favourite and is found in the *Suthon Jataka* that comes from a bigger collection called the *Pannasa Jataka*, which has echoes in the old Indian collection of

tales *Kathasaritsagara*, 'The Sea of Stories' by
Somadeva.

Its heroine, Manohra ('manohara' means
'heart conqueror' in Sanskrit) was a princess of
the kinnaras. She was exquisitely human in form
but owned light, airy, detachable wings with
which she and her similarly equipped kinnari
friends flew about the hills and dales of Himavan
between music lessons, soirées and delightful
feasts of rose petals and honeydew.

The Himavan or Snow Mountains had three
earthly levels: the Shivalik, which were the
foothills; the Himadri, which were the mid-level
mountains; and the Himachal, those mighty lords
whose snow peaks were the highest on earth,
where the gods made their camp on earth. Above
them all shimmered the celestial realm inhabited
by the demigods and heavenly beings like the
kinnaras and gandharvas.

Manohra, like all celestial maidens, was
irresistibly drawn to the beautiful lakes and lotus
ponds of the earth. Their clear, cool waters were
a physical joy that no celestial being could resist

because despite the many excellences of the celestial realm, it was earth that was blessed with sweet waters and sweet fruit.

One sun-dappled morning, after an extra-long music lesson, Manohra longed for a refreshing dip in a lotus pond. Since her friends were busy with tasks of their own she flew away by herself and taking off her wings, plunged happily into the waters. But when she stepped out humming and put on her wings again, an enormous rug of tiger skin was suddenly thrown over her, a rope quickly tied around it, imprisoning her limbs, and she felt herself being seized and borne off at great speed through the air.

On and on they flew, her kidnapper holding her light, bundled form with ease. After what seemed like a very long time, they descended to earth and Manohra heard a muffled exchange of talk before she was unwrapped.

She found herself standing on the terrace of a great and beautiful palace. A lithe, handsome, young man looked at her in wonder and so did an older man and woman, all three richly dressed and evidently noble, perhaps even royal. Manohra flung up her head and looked back at them levelly. She was not the kind to weep and beg for mercy. Instead, she cast one scornful look at her burly kidnapper, who wore the austere ochre robes of a hermit, and saluted her audience with a mannerly wai. 'I'm sure you'll tell me what this is about, good people,' she said in her low, musical voice that breathed poise and dignity. A kinnara princess had her share of backbone.

The older man and woman exchanged a fleeting glance and the woman nodded almost imperceptibly. The older man stepped forward with a charming, rueful smile.

'Welcome to my kingdom, Princess Manohra. I am King Adityavan and this is Queen Shanta Devi. This young man is our son, Prince Suthon. We asked our friend and adviser, the honourable hermit here, to seek and find an ideal bride for our son and he chose you, taking you away the moment he had the opportunity, which, as you know, is permitted on earth as a bride-seeking practice. He had observed you secretly for many days before that and tells us that not in all three realms of heaven, earth and the netherworld may a maiden be found as sweet-natured as you and as lovely and gifted in appearance and accomplishment. We trust his opinion. Will you not honour my son with your hand in marriage, now that you have been brought to us?'

The queen smiled welcomingly and looked faintly anxious. The young man stared dumbstruck at Manohra and had to be gently touched on the shoulder by his mother to recollect himself.

Manohra was a realist. She thought sorrowfully of her parents and their grief when they found her missing but knew that she was incapable just then of making her way home. She surveyed the prince through the veil of her eyelashes. 'Suthon' meant 'good arrow' and he looked properly princely and warrior-like. He had a broad, smooth forehead and a clear, steady, intelligent gaze, quite the dream prince, in fact. She inclined her head and smiled sweetly at them all.

Manohra and Suthon were married that very day and many months of perfect happiness followed, although not everyone was pleased by it. The old court counsellor brooded darkly on the slight to his own daughter, as pretty and well-brought-up as anyone could wish, whom he had indirectly advocated for months as the ideal bride for the prince, contriving to put her in the prince's way through many a gala and picnic. That, in fact, was partly why he had not succeeded, had he but known it. The prince had had suitable girls thrown at his head like cabbages and cauliflowers since he was barely in his teens and it was but natural if someone ran at you to catch you, to run away. But the old court counsellor lacked a clinical eye in the matter and only saw his ambition frustrated and hated the cause of it. 'We'll see, my fine lady . . . We'll see . . .' he muttered as he threw lucky rice at the wedded pair and took good care to appear wholly delighted.

One day, news arrived of a band of marauders attacking the border and Prince Suthon had to go off with his troops to deal with it. He told his best friend, the son of another counsellor and a junior minister at court, to keep a watchful eye on Manohra and promised to make him court counsellor when he returned. But the old court counsellor, who had the knack of eavesdropping undetected, overheard him and began to plot their doom. His chance arrived very conveniently when King Adityavan, worrying about his son, had a bad dream one night and wanted it explained the next morning in court. The old counsellor pretended to hem and haw and told him loudly with feigned reluctance and regret that it portended terrible things for the country because of the stranger in their midst. However, sacrificing the bird woman would avert all that. A fearful whisper promptly rustled through the court.

The king shot the counsellor a sharp look and said that he would consider it. Back in the royal chambers, the king consulted the queen. The queen sent at once for Manohra and explained that it was best that she disappear for a while. Sending her away to safety would free the king to checkmate the counsellor, who had cunningly made her presence seem threatening to the public.

The queen tied a silk pouch with a necklace of rubies and emeralds in it on Manohra's girdle, as a present for Manohra's mother. Flying in the face of all known classical tenets and traditions, King Adityavan and Queen Shanta Devi drew their daughter-in-law a little map, helped her fasten her wings, hugged and cried over her and got her to fly off from the royal terrace, back to her father, promising faithfully to send the prince after her when he came home. On the way out, Manohra descended briefly at the hermitage where her old kidnapper lived to take leave, and left her ruby ring with him for when her husband would come looking for her. Sure enough, the prince came back and fortified by the ring and the magic mantras that the hermit taught him, including being able to understand bird language, he took himself off to Himavan on the wings of an eagle and sent the ring to his lost lady through a maid.

Being a princess, Manohra did not want Prince Suthon to appear before her parents travel-stained, and smuggled out nice clothes for him to meet her father in. After passing a triple test of strength and skill to make the marriage legal from Manohra's father's point of view, Prince Suthon took Manohra back home and lived happily ever after. King Adityavan and Queen Shanta Devi attained immortality across the East for choosing to save their daughter-in-law instead of sacrificing her as they so easily could have done, had they succumbed to superstitious instinct. No one can tell precisely what became of the conniving court counsellor, but it's agreed that he was most probably fed to a tiger.

24

Under the pipal

Both the Mahabharata and the *Skanda Purana* tell of Barbarika. He was the son of Prince Ghatotkacha, who was the son of the Pandava prince Bhima and the lovely Hidimbi, queen of a forest kingdom in the Himalayan foothills.

Barbarika's father, Prince Ghatotkacha, was a valiant warrior and his mother was Princess Ahilavati, daughter of the serpent Bhashaka, who had found a place of honour on no less than Lord Shiva's neck.

With this pedigree, Prince Barbarika was inevitably raised to be a formidable warrior. His general education was not neglected either.

From his good-natured parents, he learnt how to speak politely to all and to restrain his natural strength in his games with other children, for he had inherited the great vigour of his father's father, Bhima. He was taught to be kind and gentle by his grandmother, Queen Hidimbi, who had stayed back to rule her kingdom and raise her son Ghatotkacha as a single mother after Bhima went home from the hills to resume his destiny as a Pandava prince in the Great Northern Plains.

Delighted by the combination of his prowess as a fighter and his gentle, knightly character, the Ashta Deva or Eight Guardians of the Directions who keep a close eye on things, decided to give Barbarika a suitable present and bestowed on him a bow with three magic arrows.

When the news came one day of the great battle likely to be fought between the Pandavas and their cousins, the Kauravas, Prince Ghatotkacha set off at once to help his father, Bhima. Soon after that came the news that the battle was a certainty and would take place on the plains of Kurukshetra, all efforts at diplomacy having failed, even those by Krishna the great Yadava prince who was cousin to both warring factions.

Barbarika asked his mother's permission to join the battle and Ahilavati agreed to let him go. But since his father, Prince Ghatotkacha, of superhuman strength had already joined the Pandavas, she wanted a promise from her son. Barbarika, being such a giant himself, should make sure to fight only on the weaker side, even if it meant fighting against his own father. That was the correct thing to do for a knight of his strength and accomplishments. Ahilavati spoke impulsively from the heart as a Naga princess dedicated to fair play and justice. Barbarika gave her his word with the most solemn oaths and promises, with the Ashta Deva for witness. Queen Hidimbi and Ahilavati blessed Barbarika and he rode away on his favourite horse, a rare blue dun, carrying his bow and three magic arrows.

A few leagues short of Kurukshetra, Barbarika stopped to rest under a large pipal tree and took a nap. When he awoke, he found himself being critically regarded by an old priest with curiously bright eyes, his white hair in a curly knot.

'A warrior with only three arrows?' said the priest to Barbarika, without even a greeting.

'Why, yes, good sir, but these are special arrows,' said Barbarika guilelessly for he was used to speaking the truth.

'What can you do with but three arrows?' smiled the priest.

'The first will fly out and mark all the targets I wish to attack. The second will mark all those I wish to save and all innocent bystanders. The third will deliver every one of my targets to me,' revealed Barbarika.

'Is that so? Do show me how they work, with all the leaves of this pipal tree,' invited the priest.

'Certainly, sir. The first and third arrows are enough for that,' said Barbarika courteously.

He shut his eyes in concentration, invoked the mantra to activate the arrows and took aim.

The first arrow flew out and marked all the leaves of the pipal tree. But the third arrow did not fly out to collect them. Instead, the first arrow flew down and hovered over the priest's foot.

'I think you have a leaf under your foot, sir. Do lift your foot before the arrow pierces you,' said Barbarika.

The priest laughed and took away his foot and sure enough, a tiny pipal leaf lay underneath that he had deliberately stepped on to test the truth in Barbarika's words. The third arrow instantly sped forth from the quiver to round up and deposit every last leaf at Barbarika's feet.

'Marvellous. So even if your opponents hide away their best warriors—say, if Krishna were to conceal the Pandavas from you, your arrows would nevertheless find them,' mused the priest. Then he asked Barbarika, 'Whose side do you intend to fight on?'

'Sir, I am pledged to my mother to always fight on the weaker side. On the way here, I heard that the Pandavas have only seven akshauhinis while the Kauravas have eleven divisions, so I intend to offer my services to the Pandavas. One of them is my grandfather, in fact,' said Barbarika.

'What?' said the priest, 'My dear young soldier, with your supernatural powers? Do you realize the consequences of your promise? I don't think you have thought it through at all and neither did your good mother, though I honour her intention.'

'Please enlighten me, sir,' said Barbarika, startled but polite.

'Whichever side you fight on will always become the stronger side. So you will have to keep switching sides to honour your promise to always fight on the weaker side. At the end of it, you will have killed everybody off, each and every person on the battlefield, and you alone will be left standing. Is that what you want to accomplish?' said the priest sternly.

Barbarika hung his head, shaken with pity and terror.

'No, sir, I do not want that,' he said.

'Best not to fight then,' said the priest and turned to leave. 'May I ask alms of you before I go?'

'Anything you please, sir,' said Barbarika at once.

'Very well, soldier, give me your head. The battle demands that the bravest warrior of all should be sacrificed before it begins, and you, undoubtedly, are he,' said the priest without losing a beat, surveying Barbarika with a challenging glint in his eye.

Shocked, Barbarika looked back at him.

'You are not what you seem, sir. Won't you tell me who you really are?' he said slowly and wonderingly with not the slightest trace of anger or revulsion at the priest's outrageous demand.

The priest raised his eyebrows faintly at that unexpected response. He cast a smile of peculiar sweetness at the gentle giant.

'Do you know me, soldier?' he said quietly and in place of the priest, Barbarika beheld the Blue God, lithe and luminous, a peacock feather in his dark, curly hair.

'Krishna,' said Barbarika, unable to say another word. His eyes overflowed and he knelt before the vision. He put out his fingertips, lifted grains of dust from Krishna's feet and put them reverently on his head.

'May I be your sacrifice, Lord,' he said and drew his sword.

'Ask something of me first, Barbarika,' said Krishna gently to the kneeling giant, placing a hand on his head.

'I have seen you, that is enough for me, Krishna', said Barbarika simply. 'And yet, I long to keep this moment always. Shyama, Dark One, please let my name be joined with yours forever.'

'So be it,' said the Blue God. 'Ask something more of me, unselfish soul.'

'I left home to do battle. But since I cannot fight, may I somehow watch its progress from a vantage point after my death?' asked Barbarika in an apologetic tone. 'My interest as a soldier consumes me. And they're family, though I've never met them.'

'Your head shall be on a hillock overlooking the plain of Kurukshetra and your soul will come to me when the battle is over and be part of me always,' promised Krishna.

And so it was.

This extraordinary legend was told thousands of years ago, yet, the people of India were unable to forget Barbarika. The thought of him went straight into their hearts and lodged there and they still dote on him and pray that he should always 'fight on their side'.

25

The orphan month

An extra month comes by in the Indian lunar calendar every thirty-two months. To be precise, it comes around every thirty-two months, sixteen days and eight ghadis, a ghadi being a unit of twenty-four minutes. The extra month was born of time to synchronize the lunar calendar, which has 354 days, with the solar calendar, which has 365 days.

Everybody knew and respected the fact that the musical beats or talas, also born of time, had names and personalities and carried the musical scales, the ragas and raginis. Just so, all the other months of the lunar calendar had names and personalities. They were in order: Chaitra, Vaisakh, Jyestha, Asadh, Shravan, Bhadra, Ashvin, Kartik, Agrahayana, Paus, Magh and Phalgun. Each month had thirty or thirty-one days and the calendar began with Chaitra on 22 March in regular years and on 21 March in leap years.

With so much to remember already, nobody had time to bother much with the extra month. They called it Adhik Maas, the Additional Month, and thought no more about it.

But the spirit of Adhik Maas minded very much. 'I don't even have a proper name,' it mourned, 'although I am witness to so much human activity, although I'm the quickstep trod between the stately measures danced by the sun and the moon. But do I belong to anybody? No, I don't. I don't belong to people. Where are my feasts and festivals? I don't belong to the sun or the moon. Have they bothered with a name for me even though I link them together? Nor do I belong to the gods up above the world so high. Do they even know I exist? It's a problem, being the thirteenth month and showing up at different times of the year, every thirty-two months, sixteen days and eight ghadis. I confuse and irritate people and they say things like, "Oh no, it's the Additional Month again. Fasts, charities and austerities! Can't do this, can't do that. Adhik Maas is a bother and a bore." I'm not unfair, I quite see their point of view and I don't exactly blame people. But I can't help feeling very low.'

One year, Adhik Maas fell between 17 June and 16 July. It should have been a happy time that year, at least for that's when the rains came and the country waited eagerly for the monsoon to blow away the dust of summer and wash everything as good as new. But the rains failed that year. The burning sun of summer seemed to reach its zenith far too soon and to stay there for an unreasonable number of hours before it reluctantly came down. The people had a terrible time for hope deferred made the heart sick. It also made stomachs sick, with food that spoilt within minutes despite being kept in cool places; it made throats sick with drinking too much cold water and it gave them all the most blinding heat headaches. Oh, how the people suffered that never-ending Indian summer. 'They're suffering doubly because of me,' thought Adhik Maas wretchedly.

'The fasts and holdbacks prescribed for my time with them are hard enough in any season. But in this terrible heat—oh, I can't bear their suffering! I'm sorry, dear people, I'm so sorry,' wept Adhik Maas. But of course, nobody could know that and poor Adhik Maas had to hear double the number of curses.

One evening, when the whole afternoon had gone by in visiting schools, homes and markets and hearing the most dreadful things about itself in angry voices of every age, Adhik Maas crept miserably to the local Vishnu temple. A crowd had gathered, washed and combed, wearing flowers and fresh clothes the way one must ideally show up in a god's house, with the right attitude of thanksgiving. Besides dropping by to greet the gods, the crowd intended to stay and hear an old pauranikar or storyteller, a famous man in the region, who was to expound the *Hari Katha* that evening at their temple. Listening to the stories of Hari or Vishnu always put everyone in a good frame of mind and the sweet smells, the gaiety and beauty of the Vaishnava temple and its excellent prasad would all be made even more enjoyable by listening to a really good story after devotions were done.

That evening, the pauranikar chose to tell the story of Bhakt Prahlad, the wonder boy saved by Vishnu. In fact, Prahlad was the only earthly being that the Blue God had personally taken an avatar for, meaning, descended on earth to save. A mere throw of his discus had saved an elephant whose foot was caught in the jaws of a crocodile, and the long flow of a magic sari had saved the Princess Draupadi from disrobing and disgrace in the cruel Kaurava court.

But he had come in person for Prahlad.

Prahlad's heart belonged only to Lord Vishnu, said the pauranikar, but Prahlad's father, the titan Hiranya Kashyap, after a long, ferocious penance, had won a boon from Lord Brahma that no weapon nor beast, man or celestial, would be able to kill him during any one of the twelve months in the year, either by day or by night, either indoors or outdoors, neither on earth nor in the air. Hiranya Kashyap wanted Prahlad to worship him, not Vishnu, and repeatedly tried to kill his son for refusing to worship another.

Vishnu was then compelled to descend in avatar for the fourth time. As Narasimha, the man-lion, at the hour of twilight, he seized and dragged Hiranya Kashyap to the threshold of his palace and disembowelled the titan on his lap with his talons. Hiranya Kashyap's dispatch took place in Adhik Maas, said the pauranikar, thus outsmarting every one of the titan's safeguards. One of the messages in this powerful teaching story is that the fates loved just such a challenge, for they disliked it very much when someone pushed the natural laws beyond a point for selfish gain.

Adhik Maas was thrilled to hear its name taken positively and loved the approving murmurs of the crowd. 'I did not know I had helped in the Lord's work,' it thought humbly. 'I'm just a unit of time. Do I even have the right to feelings?'

But then it heard something that dashed its bit of happiness to the granite floor of the temple courtyard. Somebody in the audience, a bright girl in a red skirt with two long, glossy black plaits hanging down her back, had a question.

'Every month in our calendar is dedicated to a deity, Grandfather,' she said to the pauranikar. 'Which deity does Adhik Maas belong to, please?'

'Nobody,' said the pauranikar. Talk about being publicly shamed. Adhik Maas wished passionately that it had a mortal body just so that it could dash its head on a granite pillar.

Adhik Maas lingered forlornly at the temple after everybody had gone home. It saluted Vishnu and told him sadly, 'I belong to nobody and that makes me an orphan.'

But Hari understood how it felt and said, 'You belong to me and I shall tell the priests so at Ujjain, where time is measured, this very night in their dreams that you belong to me.' And that's how Adhik Maas came to be also called Purushottam Maas or God's Month and felt at peace with eternity.

By and by, the people gave Adhik Maas a lovely festival too. The Radha–Vallabhi tradition centred in Vrindavan began to celebrate Vishnu's eighth avatar, Krishna, on the last day of Adhik Maas with 'Vyahula', the splendid allegory of Radha and Krishna's mystic marriage. The 'Vyahula' rejoiced in a happy, stress-free atmosphere with sangeet seva or an offering of music through songs, sung to the beat of a dholak drum and chimta, iron tongs, to mark the beat. Women got up and danced in joyful offerings of dance before the beautifully dressed, flower-wreathed images of Radha and Krishna. Rich and poor sat and sang cheerfully together and shared prasad afterwards.

The spirit of Adhik Maas was completely satisfied and so were the people, who really did not care for a month without a pleasant festival or two in it.

26

The bad bargains

Almost every culture has picked up on the cautionary tale of the simpleton who exchanges a thing of value for something less, and does so several times until he is left with nothing in particular. But this story stands the premise on its head.

Janba Patil and his wife, Soyara Bai, were a byword for being soft-hearted in their upland village in what is now Maharashtra. Besides a couple of fields and a few cattle, they had a small plot of land around their neat, weatherproof home, a yard full of vegetables, and gourds growing on creepers all over the fence, while a fine mango tree flourished at the back, from which hung a swing for the children. Bushes of pure white jasmine grew nearby, which Soyara Bai harvested for offerings to her household gods and to make into veni or flower-strings for her coiled hair and her daughter's looped plaits.

The tulsi or the holy basil flourished in its square, decorated brick urn in front, and the soil beneath it was silky soft, for Soyara Bai watered the tulsi every day from a copper pot as part of her daily devotions. However tired they felt after the day's chores, Janba Patil and Soyara Bai took care not to speak roughly to their little boy and girl for, said Soyara Bai, 'The hearts of children are as soft as the earth beneath the tulsi.'

Instead, they had pleasant evenings at home after Janba came home from his fields at godhuli vela, 'the hour of cow dust' as late afternoon is called in rural India because the cows come home from pasturing then in a nimbus of soft golden dust. The parents asked their children to recite the day's lessons before the evening meal. After their bellies had been fed, their heads were fed with delightful stories about the playful, mysterious gods who loved to sport with mortals for their own amusement. Especially, the children liked to hear of Krishna, a cowherd and farm boy in his childhood on earth, who loved animals and fresh white butter just as they did. The parents, too, were always glad to speak of him for they worshipped Krishna as their lord, as Vithoba of the temple town of Pandharpur.

One day, Soyara Bai told her husband, 'Why don't you sell our second buffalo at the market tomorrow? We have more milk than we need from the first one and even after I give away the excess butter I churn, I have so much left over.'

'Very well,' said Janba Patil and they washed the second buffalo down so that her skin gleamed like black silk, polished her curved horns with oil and tied a brightly beaded cord around her neck as a parting gift.

The next day, Janba led her towards a village several kos away, where cattle were usually sold. A short distance from his destination, he was hailed by a stranger on horseback.

'Where are you off to with that fine buffalo, Patil?' said the horseman.

'To sell her at the market,' said Janba cordially.

'Why bother? Why not take my fine Kathiawari mare in exchange?' offered the stranger.

'Why not, after all? My children will enjoy the rides,' said Janba and they exchanged animals. But after leading the mare away, he discovered that she was blind in one eye.

A man leading a pretty milch cow had stopped to watch as Janba gently rubbed the mare's head after she had banged blindside against a tree.

'Why not trade that one-eyed mare for my cow?' said this stranger sympathetically. Janba agreed and the stranger rode off. But a few steps forward with the cow revealed her to be lame in the hind leg. 'Never mind,' thought Janba stoutly. 'It's not your fault, poor thing,' and turned to go back to the market to see if he could sell the cow.

But a man with a goat stopped him and asked him where he was bound. 'Well, I set out to sell my fine she-buffalo, but I traded her for a mare

184

that was blind and then traded the mare for a lame cow,' said Janba.

'Why, my goat is a good deal for the cow. Trade with me,' urged the stranger and Janba agreed.

But after a short distance, the goat fell into a faint for it was very sickly. A man with a fine rooster came along as Janba hunted for herbs by the wayside to revive the poor goat and convinced Janba to trade the goat for the rooster. At last, Janba Patil arrived at the market and managed to sell the rooster for a rupee. He had planned to do some shopping after selling the buffalo but now all he had was a rupee and he found himself very hungry after his exertions along the route.

Having found the handcart man who sold zunka-bhakar, which was roti with a little dry onion curry, he looked for a place in which to eat his simple lunch. A large, shady pipal tree beckoned invitingly and Janba washed up and sat down to eat with a sigh of relief.

But just as the first morsel was on its way to his mouth, he found a man standing before him in rags, looking longingly at his food. 'Feed me, traveller. I have had no food for two days,' said the man tremblingly. Janba felt very sorry for him. He stood up at once and courteously held out his lunch. 'Eat, friend, may God keep you,' he said warmly and left to go home.

It was past the hour of godhuli when Janba Patil got home and sat down wearily on the string cot in his courtyard. Soyara Bai had long had the evening meal ready and they had all been looking out anxiously for him. The children flew to fetch water to give him to drink and to wash the dust from his face, hands and feet. 'What kept you, Baba? We were worried,' they piped and looking at their sweet, concerned faces, Janba Patil forgot how tired he was. He told them the day's adventures and apologized for coming home empty-handed.

'Not at all, you did the right thing,' said his wife. 'A horse would have been nice for the children to ride on. A cow would have been their own pet to take care of and cow's milk is very good for growing children. A goat would have been all right, too, for they say that goat's milk has healing qualities. A rooster would have made a very ornamental pet

with his fine feathers, and would have woken us up
every morning. So, all your exchanges were good.
But we didn't need that rooster. I'm glad you did
not go hungry but bought food with the rupee.'

'But I didn't eat it,' said Janba, smiling. 'I gave
my lunch to a hungry man who showed up just as
I was about to eat.'

'Well, that was right. It's good to feed the
hungry, especially if they come by when you're
eating. It's rude to eat alone without sharing,' said
Soyara Bai and the children nodded, for they had
been taught that very early in their lives by their
mother.

'You're home now, and your evening meal
is waiting,' said Soyara Bai and got up to set it
out, while the daughter fetched a cane fan with a
frilly cloth trim to wave at her father and the son
pressed his neck, shoulders and arms until they
were summoned to eat. Janba felt like the cleverest
man on earth receiving their fond attentions and
patted their heads lovingly.

The little family went off to sleep soon after,
drawing contentment like a quilt over itself.

Early next morning, they were woken up by a loud cry of 'Kokoro-ko-ko!' followed by a chorus of moos, whinnies and bleats. Lined up outside in the yard were a stout she-buffalo, a dainty bright-eyed mare, a plump she-goat in perfect health, a preening, strutting rooster and a pipal leaf on the plinth of the tulsi with a shining rupee coin on it.

'Oh!' said the children, while Janba Patil and Soyara Bai looked at everything and looked at each other.

'Now who could have brought us all these fine presents and who could those strangers on the road have been?' said Soyara Bai meaningfully, folding her hands in namaste to Vithoba, for surely it was he, their beloved god, who had made all these good things happen after testing Janba and his family to see how they responded to their bad bargains. 'Ah, who?' said Janba Patil, beaming in joy, thinking the very same thing. But the children didn't need to be told. They were flat on the ground in salute to the holy tulsi, stretched out in a full-body namaste.

27

The eldest son

This folk tale from western Uttar Pradesh, the land of the Mahabharata, tells us of a young farmer somewhere by the River Yamuna, who was very pleased with the world because he had a good-natured wife whom he loved very much and a healthy one-year-old son. But one day his wife died of a fever, and night after night, the young father walked up and down the courtyard with his weeping son on his shoulder until one evening, he thought of a ruse to calm him. He took out one of his dead wife's saris and wrapped it around the child, who was soothed by the remembered scent of his mother on her clothes and went to sleep at last, with the sari bunched against his tear-stained face.

The villagers persuaded the farmer that he should marry again, as much for his son's sake as his own. Luckily for all concerned, the second wife proved to be tremendously kind-hearted. Her name was Lata, which means 'creeper', but while she looked as pretty as a jasmine or a climbing rose, her character was like a strong, splendid tree—a sagaun or a shisham. She disdained being small-minded and took the motherless boy to be her own son from the day she first laid eyes on him. There, to that house, had she come as a bride, and everyone in it was hers. She was lucky, too, that there were no jealous old ladies or bad-tempered patriarchs in the house to put her down on principle or whose egos had to be constantly massaged.

The lady and her household throve in this encouraging situation. She presented her husband with two proofs of her affection, both sons, but so deep and absolute was her love for her eldest and so perfectly equal their treatment that the two younger sons never knew that he was a step-brother and the villagers forgot all about it as the years went by.

When the farmer died, the mother made the eldest son the head of the household and the custodian of the family's fields. The eldest son, though deeply sensitive by nature, was also possessed of a strong sense of duty. He took his responsibility very seriously, consulted the knowledgeable, applied his own ideas and took his younger brothers into his confidence in all his plans. Their homestead was a fine, well-kept house already and the eldest brother made it his purpose to maintain the cowsheds, the threshing floor and every last field and boundary and water channel in excellent order, constantly supervising, inspecting and innovating.

'A farm is a universe in itself and a mixed farm is the best thing to have,' he explained to his brothers. 'We grow staple crops and spice crops. We have a market garden for vegetables, and mango orchards. We have buffaloes, cows and goats and a large chicken run. We even have a

191

herb garden in Mother's charge, where we grow medicinal plants. She is not a lady of leisure, our mother, but as much a farmer as any of us. She is in charge of the milk, butter and ghee, in charge of making spice mixes, preserves, pickles and papads. When we take our products to the market, people must ask for the things from our village. We must get a name for quality for that is the path to success.'

The mother looked on approvingly. 'We will do well with my eldest son as the leader,' she said proudly.

The eldest son's efforts bore fruit and the family became the most prosperous in the district. The mother began to think of weddings.

But the evil eye of the villagers fell on the family. The less enterprising among them could not bear to see the family's success. They looked for a way to spoil its happiness and the second-most prosperous villager, their neighbour, remembered that the mother was really a stepmother to the eldest boy. A group of villagers got hold of the two younger brothers and told them the facts. 'He is your stepbrother after all and will certainly cheat you out of your share,' they warned maliciously.

The two younger brothers were too shocked to think straight. They found their mother alone and told her all about the villagers' warning. 'How do we stop him from dispossessing us? We'll have to kill him,' they said in hard, angry voices. They seemed to have lost their love of years for their elder brother within minutes, as a result of one conversation. The mother looked inscrutably at them, thinking her own thoughts. 'No need to have his blood on your hands. Leave it to me,' she said quietly.

That night she called out wildly, 'A snake, a snake!'

The eldest son came pounding into her room.

'Where, Mother, where?' he cried.

'It went into your stomach. Oh, my son, my son!' said the mother despairingly.

The eldest son caught his breath. 'My mother doesn't trust me,' he thought in grief, understanding her deeper meaning as he was meant to. He went back slowly to his room, his sensitive heart deeply wounded by his mother's indirect accusation of bad purpose on his part. What had made her say that when he loved her so devotedly, when everything he did was only for the welfare of the family? He could not bear the thought that his mother had the least suspicion about him. But such was his respect for her that he did not dare ask her what she meant. A hint was enough for him, as his mother knew very well.

The eldest son lost his appetite overnight and grew weaker by the day. Soon, he took to his bed and could tolerate only a bowl of thin gruel. His eyes grew dim with weeping and he turned wearily to the wall, murmuring, 'Mother, where are you?' as he had once cried without words when he was a baby.

The villagers, particularly the neighbours, were delighted. They boldly encroached on the brothers' courtyard and made a wall across the portion that they had forcibly taken away. They intruded everywhere else as well and began to next encroach on the widow's fields. The two younger brothers had neither the personality nor the courage to deal with their enemies. One day, they saw their neighbours taking a cartload of presents to the patwari, the keeper of the land records, and knew they had gone to bribe him to legalize the encroachment.

'Mother, we made a big mistake,' they said sadly. 'If our elder brother were up and about, nobody would have dared lift a finger at us.'

The mother said nothing, although it was hard not to look at them scornfully. That night she roused the house again, screaming, 'Snake!'

As usual, it was the eldest son who got to her first, even though he came limping in with great effort, holding his lamp. 'Where, Mother?' he said haltingly.

'I saw it come out of your stomach, son,' said the mother. The eldest son looked at her in silence for a long moment. He stepped closer with the lamp held high so that its light fell on her face and looked into her eyes. She looked back steadily. Her eyes made it clear that she had no suspicions about him.

'But why, Mother . . . ?' said the eldest son, the words forced out of him by his many days of agony.

'Forgive me, my child. I never doubted you. How could I ever have? But sometimes a mother has to do strange things to keep her family together,' she said very softly.

A deep sigh escaped the eldest son. He nodded and went back to his room without another word, at peace again at last.

The eldest son began to get better the very next day. Soon, he was well enough to leave his room. Seeing the wall in the courtyard, he shouted, 'Who built this?'

The neighbours looked at each other, terrified. He was back, after all. They came scampering up with spades and pickaxes and apologized as they took it down.

After a few days, the eldest son was well enough to inspect the fields. Seeing the encroachments, he roared, 'Who's trying to steal our land?'

The guilty parties came up cravenly and begged his pardon and promptly moved back to their own boundaries. They sent a messenger galloping to the patwari to hold back from tinkering with the land records.

Seeing how he made good all their losses, the younger brothers fell repentantly at the eldest brother's feet and begged his forgiveness. But his suffering had taken him to another emotional level where he no longer felt pain or pleasure with the old intensity. Even his childish, unquestioning love for his mother had a quality of detachment to it now. All he did was to pat his younger brothers absently on their heads in forgiveness while it was their mother who shed tears, looking at the two snakes born of her body, to save whom she had sacrificed the devoted love of her eldest son.

Acknowledgements

I would like to thank my first storyteller, my mother's mother, Ponni, who died many years ago, for the addictive hours of storytelling that I looked forward to eagerly as a child and pre-teen in Calcutta, Bombay and Baroda. This latter-day Scheherazade, born in the early twentieth century, was the daughter of a policeman who sent her to school wherever he was posted in the old Madras Presidency. Quite often she was the only girl in class and her desk was all by itself at a right angle to the teacher's. She hid in storybooks during breaks. She was a language fiend, fluent in Tamil, Hindi and English, and told me stories from many things that she had read and enjoyed herself: the myths of Greece and Rome, European fairy tales,

Acknowledgements

long chunks of *The Arabian Nights* and naturally,
many stories from India. She was my first bridge
between old and new India, between home and the
world.

Very particularly, I'd like to thank Vaishali
Mathur, my editor at Penguin Random House
India, who made me write this book. She chose
the title and the theme and nudged me out of
my sleepy calm, for having just written another
book, a Madrasi memoir, I was content to close
my eyes and dream away the yugas and kalpas
like Mahavishnu, or perhaps Kumbhkaran would
be a more respectful and appropriate comparison.
Once I got going, though, it was hard to stop.
Names that I was carelessly familiar with or had
had only a passing interest in became filled-out
and dynamic and 'made me tell their story', a
phrase I may have wrinkled my nose at once but
cannot now, having danced to their tune when
they chose themselves. Of course, I like them all
very much but I may as well confess that I am
secretly partial to Pingala, Satyakama, Barbarika,
Manohra, Adhik Maas, the yaksha in the lake

200

Acknowledgements

and the old curmudgeon in the tsunami story.
It was good fun, moreover, to snoop about in
old texts for ancient atmosphere. I'd like it very
much if you drop me a mail about them all at
jltyouknow@gmail.com.